GOOD OL' BOY

N. J. Edwards

ABOUT THE AUTHOR

N.J. Edwards is a writer, and the producer, director for the award winning documentary "CERTAIN ADVERSE EVENTS." N.J. enjoyed an exceptional career filming television commercials in Los Angeles and around the world. As a tabletop food specialist, N.J. knows all the trade secrets for how to make food look so appetizing on your TV screen, and why when shooting beer commercials the set smells like apple juice.

A vast rural area predisposes its relationship to the law.
Corruption finds a safe haven when few eyes are fixated.

CHAPTER 1

THE HIGHBRAND FAMILY

DEVON CLEMENT HIGHBRAND was raised in a remote part of the Appalachian Mountains. There were only about four hundred people living within a hundred miles of Devon when he was growing up. His father regularly smacked Devon and his brother Randolph around as kids to make sure they would turn out to be good ol' boys. You had to be tough and mean to be a good ol' boy, or you were a sissy, according to the elder Highbrand. Pitting his two sons against each other was Fletcher Lewis Highbrand's favorite pastime, so by the time both boys grew into young men and enlisted in the military, the brothers hated each other. But Fletcher had done what he set out to do: raised a couple of mean, tough good ol' boys.

Devon Highbrand emerged from boyhood as a boastful wannabe, often bragging to his Marine Corps buddies that he descended from the single largest landowner in the eastern colonies. If pressed on the history, Devon would spin tales of how the King of England anointed Devon's 17th-century ancestor to oversee the Mid-Atlantic mountain ranges. The ancestor was thereby gifted an enormous swath of the Appalachian Mountains. Devon would bemoan the land losses through the centuries. None of this was true.

Randolph Conrad Highbrand, having been mercilessly picked on by not only his father, but also his older brother, explained his motivations before joining the Marines: "To fly helicopters and kill gays in California." He didn't achieve the first goal, and one presumes the second is still on his bucket list. His rank was captain. He left the service after fifteen years, probably because men like this sociopath don't get promoted much beyond captain. He returned home to buy a rundown farmhouse in Pine Hill, close to his parents.

While Fletcher bullied his two sons, their mother Opal smothered them in childhood. Of the two, Randolph is the biggest mama's boy. He tells everyone, "I need a lot of side dishes with my supper." Every day you can spot his truck backed up to Opal's screen door around three p.m. She'll load up his truck bed with staples like baked hominy, garden slaw, snappy baked beans, and hickory nut cake.

Having sons was everything to Opal. She doesn't like girls. So, she had her uterus removed after giving birth to Randolph. It was a major operation in those days, and Fletcher objected, but Opal wanted to prevent the accidental birth of a daughter.

Devon's military career lasted for two decades. He spent his final few years delivering somber news to families of service members who died while on active duty. Devon is utterly opposed to women serving in the military. He thinks women are inherently inferior to men, and they pose a danger to troops. His duty forced him to sideline such sentiments when revealing news of a fallen female veteran to her grieving spouse or parent.

When Devon was denied promotion to lieutenant colonel, he was humiliated. Two women about his same age had been advanced to colonel the year he was overlooked for his O-5 rank. He bitterly toughed out the remainder of his twenty years, but not a day more. When he left the Corps, he bought sixty acres, five miles from his father and brother. He started building a house on a hilltop, which would remain barely habitable. So, during the winter months, he stuffs a wife and four kids into a small, drafty cabin that came with the land. Every couple days, they trek over to Fletcher and Opal's house to take hot showers.

The abandoned tannery that sits midway between Randolph's driveway and the turn-off to Devon's land is a reminder that for two native sons, there's no work where they grew up. Randolph tried but failed to support a wife and three kids on a captain's pension. So, he put the wife to work as a substitute teacher at the county's only high school.

Randolph's wife, the former Janice Cynthia Considine, is nice but silly. She tells people she is studying online to be a surgeon. She's attractive, and will tease Randolph when the junior and senior boys tell her she's "HOT." Randolph and Janice gave their three sons names meaning war or warrior. Gunnar, Evander, and Duncan are not favored by their grandfather. Fletcher gives all his attention to Devon's kids, often referring to Randolph's as "the stupid bunch."

When Devon returned to Pine Hill, he decided he wanted to be the county's sheriff. He has absolutely no law enforcement background or training, and doesn't care. Sheriff is an elected position. In that job, he can re-emerge as the big shot he knows he is, but believes the Corps had wrongly overlooked.

Devon, like Randolph, married his high school girlfriend. Patricia Grace Albrighton set her sights on Devon as husband material at age fourteen. Patty's favorite entry in her freshman yearbook was by her best friend Anita Linker: "Chatty Patty is the girl most likely to have Devon's babies."

Patty and Devon's four kids are Alan, Megan, and fraternal twins Charles and Catherine. Patty is delighted that with her three pregnancies she popped out one more child than Janice. She likes that her children are favored by Fletcher, although Patty doesn't care much for her father-in-law. Or, Opal for that matter.

Opal was livid that her eldest son was ensnared by an Albrighton girl. Patty was aware of her objections. Dale Albrighton was out of work much of his life. He would loaf at Harvey's Guzzle-N-Gulp in Arlodale, the next town over from Pine Hill. Most days, along with his ne'er-do-well buddies Pesky Fleming and Cubby Horn, Dale would fill the tanks of out-of-towners passing through. The Guzzle-N-Gulp's only pump was old, so gasoline would always spill out of the tank and onto the ground. Cubby used that morning's newspaper dipped in black water to clean customer's windshields. Locals would just shoo Dale and Cubby away from their vehicles. Harvey would give the three men free cigarettes. Opal hated that they'd whistle and grin at any woman who might want to stop inside for a pack of gum or a cold bottle of pop on a hot summer day.

Dale had six girls with wife Donna, but fathered two boys who were raised by other men. Dale's sons are easily recognizable. They both have his distinct cleft chin and jet-black hair with pronounced widow's peak. Patty is Dale's oldest child, and Opal thought the homeliest. Opal always kept secretly wishing for one of his other daughters to unknowingly date and marry one of her bastard brothers, but it never happened.

Devon realized he had a secret weapon in his quest to become sheriff. Megan, who's seventeen, was crowned Miss Fairs and Farms two years running. She rides from town to town, perched on the back of her boyfriend's Impala convertible as if it was a float in a parade. Her duty as pageant winner is to promote the popular county fair and annual farm council contest, where she's photographed with the prize-winning rooster for the local newspaper. Devon decided he'd follow his daughter in his pickup. At each stop, he promises his fellow citizens they'll be voting for the dad of the future Miss America. That sticks with a lot of folks whose little girls gather to see Megan in her gown and tiara.

The county's current sheriff, Angus Ungebuhler, returned home after college with a degree in criminology. He helps his father, Peter, manage their huge acreage and stock the family's farmstand in the summer. Serving as sheriff was a good chunk of Angus's income and he counted on getting elected for a second term. Out of the blue, Peter learned from Fletcher that Devon was already campaigning to unseat Angus. Fletcher knew it wouldn't only be Tanya Gambel's dry meatloaf sticking in Peter's craw at the church potluck when he stood up and declared that Devon was running for sheriff.

On election night, Devon Highbrand became the county sheriff, with a respectable 1,431 votes to Ungebuhler's 1,086 votes. With this election, any "perceived" civility that defined this county ended, at least for the time being.

CHAPTER 2

THE SPEED TRAP

ON A BITTERLY cold January morning, Ned Boone walked out his back door to find an unusual sight. Through the flurry of wet snow, he could see there was a man on top of his barn. Ned's a native of Pine Hill. After retiring as a chemical process engineer he returned home to renovate a 1900s farmhouse. His wife Ann was raised in Arlodale. Both have elderly parents living in the county.

Ned is what you'd call a gentleman farmer. He has four grazing pastures leased out, and then he gets to butcher a couple of big cows. That keeps steaks in the freezer for the whole year. Ann gardens and cans in the summer.

Ned had no idea who was on his barn's roof. He hesitated a minute before yelling at the trespasser, debating whether to go back in and grab his shotgun. His home sits just off of a state road known as Mulberry Highway. You never knew what crazies could be passing through to hunt deer or fish in the local trout streams. But while he hesitated, the intruder spotted Ned and yelled to him, "Hey, it's Deputy Cotten."

Unlike the sheriff, deputy sheriff isn't an elected position.

Deputies are chosen by the three good ol' boys on the county commission. Newly elected Sheriff Devon Highbrand would inherit two deputies, Wally Cotten and Freddy Hoover. Both men had done the job for years.

Once Ned knew who it was on top of the roof, he crossed his private lane to talk to Deputy Cotten. He saw the extension ladder leaning against the back of his barn. Deputy Cotten looked over the edge of the roof and yelled to Ned, "I'm attaching a speed trap camera to the top of your barn to catch speeders along Mulberry Highway."

Ned couldn't believe the brazenness of this character, Cotten. He realized if he'd come out of his house a minute later, he might never have noticed an apparatus attached to his barn's roof. Ned reminded the deputy, "Well, you're trespassing! I need you to remove the device and get down from my barn, immediately."

That "command" surprised Deputy Cotten. He attempted an explanation: "The speed trap is the sheriff's idea. He wants it up here." Ann Boone is Devon Highbrand's first cousin on his mother's side. Like many relations in rural areas, their families never interact. Devon just told Deputy Cotten not to get caught.

Ned was stern with his reply, which he emphatically delivered as he walked back to his house: "I don't care. Get it off and get down!" Pointing to the sky and making a circular gesture with his hand, Ned warned, "This stuff's starting to accumulate."

Ned watched from his sun porch to see Deputy Cotten drive out his lane and turn right onto Mulberry Highway. He presumed the device was gone, but there'd be no way to check for days. They were expecting two feet over the next twenty-four hours.

After he refused the speed trap installation, Ned was constantly shadowed by Deputy Cotten. Twice, Deputy Cotten ticketed a passing Ned for speeding, even though there was no proof Ned was actually speeding. So, when Ned would visit his folks up on the mountain, he'd call Ann before heading home. If she saw Deputy

Cotten patrolling, she'd alert Ned. He'd then take the winding back roads, miles out of his way, to avoid another ticket. This barn vendetta went on for a long time.

CHAPTER 3

DEBRA F. CARVER

DEVON HIGHBRAND BECAME the sheriff of a very large county. That's if you're adding up the square miles. It's about two thirds the size of Rhode Island. But, the population is small. There are no racial or religious tensions. Murders happen maybe once a decade. The opioid crisis isn't as prevalent as in other jurisdictions. So, when Devon wants an arrest, he has to swing at the lower hanging fruit: marijuana possession.

One of Devon's first arrests for drug possession was Jason Elbert Riley, age seventeen. This kid had sniffed too often around Megan. Jason is, in Devon's mind, a real yahoo who has no business pursuing a beauty queen. Megan told her dad that Jason always smokes pot behind the generator building at the high school during their free period. The possession and use of marijuana is still illegal.

Devon picked up Jason as he walked home from school on a blustery afternoon. Jason was happy to see Megan's dad pull up, thinking he was being offered a warm ride to his home, two miles away. He climbed right into the front seat of Devon's cruiser, not realizing a detour to the sheriff's office was his destination. Ebby

Riley was none too thrilled to have to drive to the sheriff's department later that night in a blizzard. His son had never bothered anybody. Ebby knew the arrest would be the gossip of the county for weeks to come.

A woman who cracked the ranks of law enforcement to become county prosecutor is Debra F. Carver. She was elected the same day as Devon. Carver and Devon butted heads immediately over the legality of Devon's methods and practices. Devon hates being countermanded and he set his sights on removing her from office. It was only four months in when Carver was caught "flipping the bird" in the direction of the new sheriff behind his back. The gesture was recorded on the ceiling camera in the sheriff's office.

Devon was angry when his arrest of Jason Riley was denied prosecution by Carver. The kid was busted with just two fat joints. There was no justifiable cause to pick him up in the first place. Carver thought it was inappropriate to consider this arrest for prosecution and dropped the charges.

That's when Debra F. Carver's days became numbered. It didn't take too many encounters for Devon's verbal abuse to elicit the middle finger. Then it was another two months for the ethics disciplinary board to make a determination about Carver's obscene gesture. And then, "poof," she was gone. She even uprooted her two young kids and left the county. Devon couldn't believe his good luck. He thought he'd have to work a lot harder to get rid of her.

When Carver's tenure as prosecutor ended abruptly, a man named George Lee Welton III became county prosecutor. He had just held the position before Carver. He made a bid in the last election for state's attorney, but lost. He didn't really want the county prosecutor job again, but took it anyway. Welton served the county years ago as a deputy sheriff, before going back to law school. Welton's the exact type of ethically challenged good ol' boy Devon knows he can get along with.

CHAPTER 4
BEER GUT "BOB"

ABOUT THIRTY MILES from Pine Hill is Sizemore, the county seat where the sheriff's office and jail are located. The few attorneys in the county reside there. Ethical lawyers usually try to score side jobs as attorneys for the farm council or county commission. The unethical lawyers run various scams to survive.

Quincy Robert "Bob" Merson loves a good scam. A thrice loser in marriage and for elected positions around the county, Merson insists on his nickname, "Bob," being in quotation marks, even in court filings.

Merson did his stint in the Army in Texarkana. He tried really hard to be a cowboy during those days in the service. On weekend leave, he tried roping and bronco busting. But he ruptured a nut bull riding in what he believed was a PBR qualifier. It turned out the venue where he forfeited the family jewel was nothing more than a Texhoma sideshow with no permits. After his Oklahoma lawyer took almost half of Merson's $20,000 for pain and suffering, "Bob" decided he'd become a lawyer.

Forty years later, he still wears a cowboy hat and a cowboy-themed button-down opened to his beer gut. Only in court will he remove the hat, and only when asked. Around his neck is a solid gold medallion shaped like a branding iron that spells "BOB," complete with the quotation marks.

Twice Merson lost a bid for county commissioner. But the defeat that hurt the most was when he was beaten by Debra F. Carver for county prosecutor. He helped Sheriff Highbrand get rid of Carver by writing several scorching complaints about her job performance to the ethics disciplinary board. In one of them he sank so low as to accuse her of stealing office furniture.

After Carver was eliminated, Merson convinced the morally malleable Sheriff Highbrand to go along with his profitable grifting scam. The idea was to target poorer decedents who die in the county with no last will and testament. They soon had their first victim.

When a widowed Mrs. Jake Lovell passed away at age seventy-nine without a will, her estate had to go to the sheriff of the county to administer. Understanding the monetary rewards of Merson's scheme, Devon suggested that Merson should do the appraisal of the estate to expedite the settlement.

Devon explained to the decedent's son, Harry Lovell, "Your mother's estate can't be closed unless a thorough appraisal is submitted to the county clerk by my department. You can't claim her possessions or sell anything off until that's done. I don't have the staff to handle estate settlements."

Harry figured all of his mom's worldly goods would net less than $35,000. He signed his contract with Merson. Merson's fee is five percent of the final appraised value of the estate. Once Lovell signed on the dotted line, Merson increased the value of everything. For Mrs. Lovell's estate, Merson's appraisal was $98,000 not the actual $35,000. His fee with expenses was $5,000.

It didn't matter to Merson that Mrs. Lovell won't leave behind an estate valued at $98,000. He has pages and pages of suspicious auction receipts and other documentation to show a judge, if need be. He'd claim Grandma's survivors are too dumb to get top dollar for her stuff.

Appraisals are kept just under $100,000, so as not to trigger automatic probate court. The goal is to acquire as much as possible in jacked up appraisal fees for Merson and Devon to split. Merson needs a willing sheriff to carry out the scam. Devon was hooked when this first side hustle of the Lovell family put $2,300 in his pocket.

CHAPTER 5
TWO MILLION DOLLARS

PATTY IS IN her heyday as Mrs. Sheriff, too. Through the years she somehow managed to get a degree in social work. When she and Devon moved back to Pine Hill, she got a job counseling addicts. It involved too much travel around the region. So, she had Devon create a paid position for her, strictly within his county. She is the social worker for those on home reporting probation. The county commission had a hard time approving funding for this opportunistic nepotism. However, they scraped together a small salary for Patty's services, so as not to antagonize Devon.

Patty's flush with cash, anyway. Before Devon became sheriff, his Aunt Lois relocated to Pine Hill from Washington, D.C. As soon as Lois set foot in Pine Hill, Patty tapped her for a $50,000 "loan." Patty said she needed the money for her kids and their upcoming college expenses. In actuality, Patty would use the cash to hire a builder to finish her hilltop dream home. She never again wanted to stay in that drafty winter cabin.

Lois Fleetwood's a moderately wealthy woman with a fifty-year-old daughter who lives with her. The daughter, Mallory, was born with intellectual and developmental disabilities. Colonel Malcolm Fleetwood died when Mallory was young and Lois never remarried. Lois and Malcolm had purchased a home near the Potomac. After selling her property, Lois's net worth topped two million dollars.

Lois and Mallory moved back to Pine Hill because Opal succeeded in luring her sister home. Opal insisted they'd do everything together. She'd cook up a storm, and they'd enjoy gathering every Sunday for big family suppers, just like when they were kids.

Fletcher had no intention of sitting at his supper table, on any given Sunday, across from an odd duck like Mallory Fleetwood. But he had enough land for Lois to bring in a new manufactured home and dig a well. That's if she cared to pay off the remainder of the mortgage on his four acres, which was only about $25,000. Lois Fleetwood's return to Pine Hill was the closest thing the Highbrands had to hitting the jackpot. And none of them can stomach the fact that Mallory will someday inherit Lois's millions.

CHAPTER 6
THE PROSECUTING DICK

BETTY BRAEDON WORKS for an insurance company in Sizemore. Her husband's gone a lot, working two states away as a pit boss at a casino. He's home Mondays and Tuesdays, but the rest of the time, Betty is all alone with her only son, Theo. Theo Braedon caught the attention of the sheriff's department at age thirteen. At seventeen, he deals small amounts of powder and pills.

Theo Braedon's only source is Jeremy Wilfong, a nineteen-year-old Floridian Theo met snowboarding at the Ridgecrest Ski Runs. Wilfong couriers bags of pills and cocaine through Sizemore, on his way to a northern college from his home in south Florida. The pills are provided by a couple of goofs who work in Miami nursing homes, stealing old folk's medications. Theo feels quite sophisticated for his area, even though he is mostly dealing in geriatric pharmacology like Valium. But he recently scored a trove of Dilaudid pills. His mother realizes Theo is risking a potential new arrest and prosecution.

Betty experienced an encounter with Prosecutor George Lee Welton III that she never told anyone about, not even her husband.

Occasionally, she'll see Welton around town, and he acts like he doesn't even know her. Surely he hasn't forgotten what he'd done? Betty knows, someday, she'll blow the whistle on Welton. She just wants Theo to be away at college and out of the county before she does.

When Theo was arrested at thirteen for tagging businesses up and down Main Street, Welton scheduled a meeting for Betty to come to his office. She left work at noon on a Friday, during her one-hour lunch break. Welton said he wanted to talk about her son's arrest. He sympathized with Betty, as Theo was her only child. He had obtained the child's school records, and told Betty how impressed he was that Theo had done mostly A and B work in elementary school. He even joked about how colorful and expressive the graffiti was, and said her son had an artistic talent that could be developed. Betty wasn't amused.

Then the conversation switched to the absence of Betty's husband, Tom. Welton probed further into the home life of the three Braedons. Betty was becoming uncomfortable with Welton, as he asked, "How much of the time is Theo without his father?" Betty looked through the glass window of Welton's office and saw that his staff had probably gone to lunch. Soon, Betty would need to head back to her office. She heard her stomach growling.

As Welton noticed Betty fidgeting, his cordial tone changed. He told Betty there was a good possibility that Social Services would be removing Theo from her home. Welton said, "I might recommend that Theo spend the next eighteen months in a juvenile detention facility. There doesn't seem to be enough discipline in your own home for your young teen." Welton reminded her that there were multiple damaged businesses, and the likelihood of recidivism is high. Welton advised, "I don't want to throw the book at Theo. But, on the other hand, a stiff penalty for your son will send a clear message to other teens and parents."

As Betty pled the case that her son wouldn't harm the community again, Welton approached Betty and stood over her. He told her he was willing to be nice to her kid, but she had to do something for him. Was Betty willing to negotiate? Welton told Betty her son could go free if he could place his penis in her hand. He asked her, "Would that be alright?" That was all she had to do, he said. Just hold his penis in her hand and her son would go free.

Betty couldn't believe what he was saying. Welton sternly asked, again, "Do you want your son to go free?" Betty meekly nodded in the affirmative. Welton quickly unzipped his trousers and pulled out a limp penis. He forcibly took her right hand and placed his penis across her palm. He held tight to her wrist, for thirty seconds or so, as Betty looked away. He then let her go, zipped up his trousers, and told her, "You can pick up the paperwork on Monday."

CHAPTER 7
KATY LEGONICK

SOME EIGHTEEN MONTHS after Devon became sheriff, two twenty-something women found themselves on home reporting probation. One woman, Katy Legonick, wasn't arrested by Devon, but had moved to his county before her sentencing began. She's an addict from over in Flintville, an unincorporated town in neighboring Beasley County.

Katy had been in and out of jail as a teenager due to an abusive home life. She has been given an opportunity, through a vocational rehabilitation program, to work at a Mennonite dairy on the outskirts of Sizemore. The other woman, a local, Livia Ellen Bangertt, was arrested for possessing two ounces of marijuana and a variety of unprescribed narcotics when her car was searched by Deputy Cotten during a traffic stop.

Home reporting probation is primarily a go to work, then home, sentencing deal. It requires no slip-ups, or one could find themselves back in jail. Patty has these two new clients to visit. She'll either do surprise pop-ins on the weekend, or scheduled visits on a weekday if the person has a full-time job. Patty prefers weekend visits. She'd rather be at home with her husband and kids at night, and her kids and husband want nothing to do with her on the weekend.

Katy doesn't know too many people in Sizemore. She rents a one-bedroom apartment above the hardware store on Main Street. When Patty knocked on her door on a sticky summer afternoon, she expected to be let in right away. Instead, it took a few minutes of Katy yelling, "I'll be right there," before Katy opened the door.

A perspiring and annoyed Patty entered the apartment. Katy looked high to Patty. All the windows were open, as if to air out the smoke. Two guys were seated at the kitchen table. Katy introduced Lou and Eric: "These are my friends from over in Flintville."

Patty had met twice before with Katy, but kept this visit short. The heat and humidity was now inside Katy's apartment. Katy was quizzed about the job, her mental state, and whether or not she'd been clean. Job was good, mental state good, and yes, she'd stayed clean.

Patty gathered up Katy's home reporting logbooks, and left. Katy hoped she had convinced Patty that everything was okay. As Katy closed her apartment windows, Lou reminded Katy to whom Patty is married by stating the obvious. "The sheriff's going to hear about this."

CHAPTER 8
MARIJUANA FIELDS FOREVER

THE MONDAY AFTER Patty told Devon that Katy Legonick was high during her home reporting probation visit, Devon took a call from State Senator Curtis Ray Milford. A Franklin Logging Company caravan had arrived at a staging site for a timber operation on top of Dowd's Peak. Milford's office was apprised they found mature marijuana plants growing throughout the trees that were coming down. Milford needed to tell the logging company what to do. Did the sheriff's office or feds need to see it as evidence? Should he call the state police? Devon told Senator Milford, "I'll handle everything."

This was interesting news for Devon. Pot growers had eluded his sheriff's department. He and Deputy Cotten immediately high-tailed it up the mountain. Estes Durbin's land borders state land near the clear cutting site, and Durbin's dirt access road brought them to the top of this peak. The timber operation was about a mile from there.

Estes Durbin's clan had claimed land on Dowd's Peak in the mid 19th century, but settled in the valley below for well water. A brittle cabin someone built is falling over. Thick forest surrounds the cabin, with young tree shoots growing inside.

Devon noticed a substantially worn, wide path through the trees from the top of Durbin's dirt road. He and Deputy Cotten took the path. About fifty yards in, the landscape opened up to a hillside full of marijuana. The array of plants cascaded down the mountain, catching the bright sun. This was not what Senator Milford had described as marijuana growing throughout the woods at the timber site. This was a large planted field.

The tall female plants Devon inspected had been pruned recently. They had received lots of summer sun and enough rain. Devon marveled at what he'd stumbled upon: "These growers know what they're doing." He explained to Deputy Cotten, "The soil on this hillside is really rich from decades of sheep grazing and centuries of decomposing forest mulch." After scanning the entire field and taking in its expanse Devon continues, "They'll be harvesting soon. It could frost up here by Labor Day."

Devon's first call when they got back down the mountain was to Prosecutor Welton about the discovery. Gleefully, Devon relayed the news, "George, you're going to have a big bust to prosecute!" He detailed to Welton his conversation with Senator Milford and described the extent of the huge marijuana field.

Estes Durbin is over ninety years old. He has two living daughters, grandchildren, and great-grandchildren. Devon wonders if his kin are responsible for this magnificent crop. Who would have the audacity to set up such a risky enterprise on a stranger's land? But he didn't want to call Estes just yet.

Early Tuesday, Devon and Deputy Cotten took the long way around the mountain to get to the clear cutting site. The Franklin Logging Company foreman, Larry Stoll, was told to notify the sheriff if anyone else showed up asking questions. Away from the lumberjacks, Devon and Deputy Cotten explored some of the marijuana growing throughout the forest. The feral plants in between the trees were really tall. Some had shot up to over nine feet trying to get a share of sunlight from beneath the forest's canopy.

Back at Durbin's cabin, Deputy Cotten mounted a surveillance camera to spot any vehicles coming up Durbin's road. There was no signal on the mountain. Cotten would have to manually check the surveillance every forty-eight to seventy-two hours. On the drive back to the sheriff's office, Devon floated the idea of setting up a sting.

CHAPTER 9

INFORMANT TORMENT

KATY LEGONICK ARRIVED home from her shift at the dairy at four-thirty p.m. on the Tuesday after Patty's visit to find a deputy sheriff's cruiser parked in front of the hardware store. The vehicle was empty. She hoped it was just an off-duty cop who needed house paint or light bulbs. As she pulled around the corner of the building to her parking spot, there was a uniformed deputy leaning against the steps to her apartment. Katy was scared. She didn't want to go back to jail. She had the instinct to flee.

Deputy Cotten smiled at her as she parked a couple feet from where he was standing. He asked through her open passenger side window, "Will you please step out?" He informed her he was there on official police business, but not to arrest her. Katy reluctantly emerged from the car. Deputy Cotten gestured with his arm that they go upstairs. He gave her the once over as she walked ahead of him to her apartment, commenting, "Your butt looks good in those jeans."

Once inside Katy's apartment, Deputy Cotten got Devon on the phone and put him on speaker. The sheriff introduced himself.

He explained that his wife will be reporting to the magistrate that Katy is still using, in violation of her sentencing deal.

Katy admitted to the sheriff, "My friend Lou brought some weed to my apartment, but I didn't smoke any, just my friends did."

Devon knew this was a lie, but let it slide. Any illegal substances on the premises are a violation of home reporting probation. Devon told her, "The report by my wife can be removed from your file if you voluntarily work with my sheriff's department. I'll also cancel your drug testing."

Deputy Cotten stared at Katy as she stared into his cell phone. He smiled when he noticed a small butterfly tattoo on her neck. Her auburn hair was in a ponytail, cinched by a purple band. A few strands that escaped the purple band were falling around her face. Cotten wondered what she did at the dairy all day. She didn't smell like sour milk.

Devon explained, "Deputy Wallace Cotten is going to give you instructions that you'll need to follow carefully. If you agree to the terms, you'll be my confidential informant, indefinitely. Nothing will interfere with your work at the dairy."

Katy looked at Deputy Cotten. He was nodding and grinning. She asked into the phone, "What will I have to do?"

Devon said, "Everything will be run through Deputy Cotten. There's no need for me to contact you again. Do you understand the opportunity I'm proposing?"

Katy said, "I understand. I want to stay out of jail."

Deputy Cotten said to Devon, "I'll take it from here, Sheriff." Cotten ended the call then asked Katy, "What do you have to drink? I'm thirsty!"

CHAPTER 10

THE MILKMAN

LOIS FLEETWOOD HAS resided in Pine Hill for a few years without any trouble involving her daughter. But a man named Earl Pape has taken an interest in Mallory, and unfortunately, Mallory is reciprocating. Lois never encountered this dilemma before. Pape is in his early fifties. Mallory has never been on a date.

Earl Pape works at the Mennonite dairy and delivers milk to the surrounding towns. He changed his dairy truck route to coincide with the time of day Mallory volunteers at the Pine Hill men's club hall, serving lunches for the indigent and disabled. The lunch cook on Thursday, Michele Hockaday, caught Mallory and Earl kissing behind the building. Michele broke up the encounter. She immediately called Lois.

Michele told Lois that there'd been a flurry of gossip through-out the hall when Mallory came inside crying. Old Bruiser Uhler told Michele that Earl Pape had kidded with him about Mallory a few times. Regarding Mallory's future inheritance, Earl Pape said to Bruiser, "One day that will all be mine."

After Michele told Lois what Pape said about Mallory, Lois

knew some changes had to be made for herself and her daughter. Lois is fed up with all the Highbrands, too. Month after month she's had to ask Patty to make payments on her loan. Patty rarely complies and dodges any run-ins with Lois around Pine Hill. Lois knows her money went toward finishing Devon and Patty's house, not college tuition.

Fletcher died of a sudden heart attack a couple months before the Earl Pape situation presented itself. Lois supported her grieving sister during that horribly upsetting time. But Opal still doesn't want to be with Lois and Mallory, even though Fletcher's gone. She only spends time with her sons and their sons. Opal comes by to visit with Lois when she's a little short on cash for the heating oil bill.

Lois ended Mallory's dalliances with the milkman. She recalled saving a brochure about a new retirement community about an hour and a half away in Beasley County. The brochure depicted modern cottage-style living, a dining hall and beautiful secured grounds with a swimming pool. The place was named the "Terrace Residences in Perryville." She asked Ann and Ned to drive her and her daughter over there the following weekend. Mallory loved the place!

CHAPTER 11

THE FINN TRAP

DEPUTY COTTEN IS prancing around Katy Legonick's apartment, getting a feel for the place. His girlfriend Ramona Beverage is a constant nag. He thinks Katy is damn cute and she's young. He likes young. Ramona is thirty-four with a bunch of baggage. As he walks through Katy's bedroom, touching her stuff and looking out the window, he's fantasizing about places he can go with Katy on a date. Meanwhile, he'll be spending time with her on this marijuana bust. Settling himself comfortably on Katy's couch, Deputy Cotten asks, "Do you know Livia Bangertt?"

Katy asks, "Why?"

Cotten explains, "I arrested Livia Bangertt several months ago. She gave up the person she gets her grass from. That dealer has been arrested." He emphasizes to Katy, "That made the sheriff really happy. Do you want to tell me who you're getting your grass from?"

Katy's nervous around this deputy. He gives her the creeps. She doesn't know what Devon knows. Allegations of sex crimes have been leveled against Wally Cotten through the years. Katy tells

Deputy Cotten, "I'm not getting grass or any drugs from anyone. I slipped up letting my friends smoke here."

Cotten likes how nervous Katy is acting as she speaks. It's giving him a chub. He tells Katy, "You're going to be part of a sting operation. Livia's longtime dealer is a guy named Finn Galford. Do you know him?"

Katy shakes her head. "No."

Cotten briefs his newly acquired C.I. on the target of the sting. Finneas Arlo Galford is thirty-one years old, has been in the service, and lives in Arlodale with no obvious means of support. He rents a double wide at Spark's Trailer Park. His people have been in Arlodale going back generations. His great-grandfather Arlo Kern, Jr. and Estes Durbin's father, Henry, opened the Durbin and Kern Tannery in the early twentieth century. Arlodale is named after Arlo Kern, Sr.

Cotten explains to Katy, "Everyone around knows Finn Galford deals weed. His customers just pull up to his trailer and honk. That's how I nabbed Livia. She was pulling out of Spark's Trailer Park. The sheriff doesn't suspect Finn of planting the big field of marijuana up on Dowd's Peak. But, it might be where his stash comes from."

Katy interrupts Deputy Cotten. This is the first time she's hearing about why they are setting up a sting operation. She asks, "There's a big field of marijuana up on the mountain?"

Deputy Cotten continues, "Yes. Sheriff Highbrand wants to know what Finn knows. This is where you come in. The growers planted the marijuana on Mr. Durbin's land, and Finn Galford used to be tight with the Durbin family."

Deputy Cotten goes on to outline the mechanics of the sting. He'll pick up Katy at eight p.m. on Friday and drive her to Arlodale, to the bridge at West Run Creek. There, she'll meet up with Brian Hager. Hager is a twenty-five-year-old who has done narc undercover since he was nineteen. Hager has never met Finn.

The night of the sting, Hager and Katy will pop by Finn's trailer and honk. It's Friday and Hager's looking to party with his girlfriend. After asking to buy enough weed for the weekend and offering a cold six-pack, they'll get an invite to go inside Finn's trailer.

Katy's prepped that she doesn't need to do any of the talking. Deputy Cotten tells her, "You're basically arm candy. After a night of hanging out, you'll be welcomed back to Finn's at any time, without us paying Hager."

Katy asks Deputy Cotten, "Am I allowed to smoke and drink while I'm at Finn's?"

The answer from Deputy Cotten: "Of course!"

Deputy Cotten leaves Katy's apartment and notifies Devon that their C.I. is prepped. Devon has prepped the narc. Both men are extremely amped-up, as neither has done anything like this before. For Devon it feels like real cops and robbers stuff to execute a sting operation. He believes with this huge bust on the books he could be primed for some notoriety and a higher political office. Maybe he'd challenge Curtis Ray Milford for his position.

The narc is provided by George Lee Welton III. When Devon alerted Welton he was going to have a big bust to prosecute, Welton contacted a state police buddy from over in Geyerton. Lieutenant Ronald Hayle had made a name for himself a couple years back when he busted a bootleg fentanyl ring. Brian Hager was the undercover buyer.

On the big night, after handing Katy off to Hager at West Run Creek, Cotten hooks up with Ramona for an hour. The thought of seeing Katy again, combined with a couple stiff shots of bourbon, makes the usually prosaic sex with Ramona the best quickie Cotten's had in months. At eleven p.m., Cotten jolts out of bed and tells a perplexed Ramona he's leaving.

Cotten can't get Katy's smell out of his mind. He hopes the essence of floral she exuded when he brought her from Sizemore to

Arlodale isn't replaced by the stench of marijuana on her clothes. Cotten never smoked anything and doesn't like the smell of pot or cigarettes on a woman.

At midnight, Hager briefs Deputy Cotten in person and Devon on speaker phone. He hands over the grass he purchased. There's nothing much to tell, from Hager's perspective. The cover story he told Finn was that Katy's cousin is a forklift operator with Franklin Logging. During a recent clearcut job, the company found wild weed growing all over the top of Dowd's Peak. Hager says, "Finn inquired about the location of the logging operation and that was about all. He said he used to go up on Dowd's Peak all the time as a boy, but hadn't been there in years. He also didn't say where on Dowd's he used to go. He seemed genuinely surprised there was feral weed up there. He didn't give any clue that he was aware of a planted field."

Devon asks, "Were you the only two people with Finn?"

Hager replies, "Yes! Nobody came by while we were there."

Devon asks, "Did he say where he gets his weed?"

Hager replies, "Finn did tell us his grass is homegrown as he was sparking a bowl. But he didn't say anything about a supplier. It was good stuff, though." Hager looks at Katy for agreement and asks, "Right?"

Katy smiles at Hager and nods in the affirmative that the grass is good stuff. To Deputy Cotten she says, "I just had a couple hits." Deputy Cotten puts his hand on Katy's shoulder. She still smells like flowers. He thinks gardenia, maybe. Katy brushes his hand away.

Hager finishes his recap. "Finn did say he was going to go check out Dowd's Peak and grab some of the plants for himself. As a cover, I asked Finn to cut down a few plants for me, too, if he could. Finn said he would."

Devon congratulates Hager on a job well done and thanks Katy, too. Hager takes off. Katy gets in the passenger seat of Deputy

Cotten's cruiser. There's soft music playing. Cotten tells Katy, "You did great!" He asks, "Would you like to grab a drink at my place?"

Katy wants to get back to her apartment as fast as possible. She'd actually had a really fun night with Hager and Finn, and smoked a lot more than a couple of hits. She makes the excuse, "I drank some beer and didn't eat anything. I'm feeling kinda sick. Can you just take me home?"

Deputy Cotten suggests he can whip her up some scrambled eggs and bacon at his place. He mentions, "I'm just a couple miles from here. You'll feel better if you eat something!" Trying to sound friendly and lighthearted he quips, "The night is young!"

In a snarky tone, Katy asks, "Am I off work now?"

That last question really pierces through Cotten's lighthearted-ness. He stares ahead at the road and doesn't answer. They're both silent on the long drive until they get to her apartment. Then the deputy yells out a reminder to Katy as she goes up her apartment steps: "You're my C.I. indefinitely."

CHAPTER 12
WHERE THERE'S A WILL

As Lois prepares to vacate the land she parceled from Fletcher and move into a two bedroom cottage at the "Terrace Residences in Perryville," the Highbrands have varying reactions to Lois leaving Pine Hill. Opal won't talk to her. Patty is thrilled. Randolph wants Lois to leave her home furnished, to rent short term to hunters. He promised he would make Lois a good income renting the house. She declined his offer, listing the place for sale immediately. That pissed off Randolph and upset Janice who would like to quit substitute teaching.

Lois had made that mistake before. When she first moved back to the country, she bought an investment condo near the Ridgecrest Ski Runs. It's a beautifully furnished, one-bedroom condo that sleeps four, in a recently built, rustic complex with a view down the mountain. Randolph promised Lois he'd keep investment income flowing with year round short-term rentals to skiers in the winter, and off-roaders in the warmer months. She paid him a commission the few times he got it rented to winter tourists. But after the first thaw it sat vacant all spring. So, eventually, Lois rented it full time to a Ridgecrest Lodge manager and his wife.

The trust fund Lois designed for Mallory's inheritance needs revisions. When she moved to Pine Hill, at the urging of Fletcher and Opal, she appointed Devon and Randolph to be trustees of the trust fund. She no longer wants her nephews in charge of Mallory's future finances.

Lois picked a new trustee for Mallory's trust fund. It is a bank with a five star rating for investment products. To hell with relatives! Leeland Culp is the Vice President for Financial and Investment Services for Pinion Echo Bank and Trust. It was times like these Lois wished she was still in a big city, instead of inside some rural bank branch with bull roast flyers taped to the front door. There's a water cooler in the corner. Are those still a thing?

Mr. Culp is very pleasant. Lois details the special needs of Mallory. They discuss an approach that will take care of her daughter for the rest of her natural life. He refers Lois to a female attorney in Beasley County whom she likes very much. All Lois has to do is get the trust fund document written for both of them to sign.

CHAPTER 13

BIG BADGE AND LITTLE BADGE

AN ANONYMOUS PINE Hill blogger emerged. They're engaging a good number of people. Patty is engaged, too. Every day she tries to figure out who is responding, with thumbs up, to the nasty posts about her husband.

The blogger uses nicknames for his subjects. Devon is "Big Badge," Wally Cotten is "Little Badge," and "Bob" Merson is "Beer Gut Bob." Patty wanted an explanation from Devon when the blogger posted a mysterious rant titled "Big Badge and Beer Gut Bob in cahoots for dead people's loot."

Devon made sure Patty wasn't aware of his side gig with "Bob" Merson. The jacked-up appraisal fees that net Devon extra cash are paid directly to Merson. Devon hides his take from Patty. His money's literally hidden in a plastic gallon storage bag in an old paint can and buried under his drafty cabin. Now, out of nowhere, this blogger is indicating a knowledge of Devon's partnership with Merson. Devon immediately tells Merson they have to cool the grift.

Patty is anxious about Devon, anyway. Her husband and the Beasley County Sheriff share magistrates and judges. All of that trial work moved from Sizemore to Perryville, the county seat in Beasley County. Devon is gone a lot more. Their relationship is strained. Patty's worried about their marriage.

The Pine Hill blogger goes by the name General Sherman's Ghost. General Sherman's Ghost suddenly announced there's a mountaintop of wild marijuana growing on Dowd's Peak. In the posting about this interesting discovery, GSG nicknamed the mountain "Cannabis Crest." Devon wondered if General Sherman's Ghost was Finn.

The surveillance camera on Durbin's cabin caught Finn snooping around, then heading off into the forest down the path that leads to the grow operation. A day later, Finn came back with two other men Devon knows. They parked at the top of Durbin's access road for a couple hours. When they left, Finn carried a stuffed burlap sack. Devon figured there'd be others snooping around after the recent blog. It would be harder to spot the actual growers from nosy looky-loos.

Devon informs Finn he was caught on surveillance and has him in for questioning, along with Jackson Dillard and Caleb Ungebuhler. The sheriff asks Finn, "How do you know about Estes Durbin's road on Dowd's Peak?"

Finn tells Devon, "I used to go to Durbin's cabin when I was a kid."

Devon asks, "What was in the big burlap sack?"

Finn wisecracks, "I decided I'd start collecting pine cones."

Devon asks, "Are you the blogger who told everybody there's marijuana growing up there?"

Finn replies, "I am not! It's General Sherman's ghost!"

Dillard and Ungebuhler have nothing to share except a few more wisecracks. Other than trespassing on Durbin's land, they aren't guilty of anything.

Devon discusses with Prosecutor Welton if they should wait a while longer to try and nab the growers. Welton insists they should. But Senator Milford had seen the Pine Hill blogger's blog about "Cannabis Crest" and nixes the idea of waiting. Arrangements are made with the feds for the field to be sprayed and destroyed the following week. Devon finally calls old Estes Durbin to tell him what's going on at his mountain property.

Estes asks, "Is the cabin still there? Daddy built it in 1910 when he had a herd of sheep grazing on the mountain. Marybeth and I had some good times in that little shack! Doreen was conceived up there." Estes chuckles!

Devon replies, "It isn't much more than a few rickety boards."

Estes has a good laugh when Devon mentions the forest of wild weed. He remarks, "I wish it was growing wild when I was young. I could've made a buck." Estes answers Devon's inquiry about his kin planting the field, "I haven't seen any of them in a couple of years. They don't like the country." Ending the call, Estes says, "When I'm gone, my girls can fight over the few acres on that old mountaintop." He laughs a big belly laugh and hangs up.

Devon instructs Deputy Cotten to go ahead and remove the camera from Durbin's cabin. "I don't want to see Charley or Cathy on the surveillance," Devon tells Cotten. Randolph's two younger sons Evander and Duncan were just recorded snooping around. The mountain is now a teen destination.

Cotten asks, "What about Katy Legonick? I think she should go back to Finn Galford's to pick up the marijuana plants that he promised the narc."

Devon agrees, "You're right. If she doesn't, Finn might get a bad feeling about Hager. Tell her, once she goes to Finn's, she's released from her C.I. role."

CHAPTER 14
FRESH MINT

DEVON MET A woman named Mint Brisbee. She works at the Beasley County Courthouse in Perryville. She was born Arminta Lucille Brisbee, but everyone calls her Mint. She's around twenty years younger than Devon. Patty is right to be worried about her marriage, because things between Devon and Mint are heating up.

Devon planned to head over to Perryville, early Saturday morning, for a rendezvous with Mint. He told Patty he was meeting with the feds up on Estes Durbin's property to discuss the spraying of herbicide, which is to begin on Monday.

Before he can escape the house, Patty asks Devon, "Why are you in civilian clothes if you're meeting with the feds? And why are you wearing your new sweater if you're walking around through the messy forest? Why did you tell Charley he can't have the truck if you're in the cruiser all day?" Devon had no answers for any of this.

Devon had only ever been with Patty and one other woman. When he was stationed in Maryland, he had a brief fling with Megan's piano teacher. It didn't last long, as both were married. Patty never knew about that affair, but Devon isn't sure he'll be hiding anything again. He knows, deep down, things with Patty are finished. They have been for some time.

Mint is unmarried, but there is still no place she and Devon can chance going in public. He picks her up around the corner from her apartment. She lives on a quiet side street three blocks from the courthouse. She laughs about the cruiser. She asks Devon, "Do you want to handcuff me? Should I sit in the backseat?"

Devon's embarrassed that Patty cornered him before he left home and forced him into the cruiser. It makes it harder to hide his whereabouts. Mint understands. He heads away from town to the first dirt turnoff road. They drive until the cruiser is swallowed up and hidden by the dark woods. They kiss passionately for several minutes and linger in each others arms before driving to Dowd's Peak. Devon wants to show her the big marijuana field.

CHAPTER 15

AMELIA

Lois's niece, Amelia Etchison, is visiting Lois and Mallory in their new town of Perryville. Amelia runs a successful business firm based in San Diego with two other women. Etchison, Scherr & Munford develops management strategies and does hiring for private startups across the country. Amelia's mom, Evelyn, was Lois's older sister and best friend. When they were young women, Evelyn and Lois moved together to Washington, D.C. to look for work. They both married Army officers and each had one child. Amelia and Mallory grew up together.

Amelia is also still close with her cousin, Ann Boone. As kids, Ann and Amelia were two peas in a pod. Evelyn would bring her only daughter to visit her grandparents for a month each summer. Ann and Amelia would run from morning to night throughout the safe countryside in Arlodale.

Mallory already began volunteering for the dining hall staff at the Terrace Residences, just as she had done in Pine Hill. This is great for Mallory and for Lois.

The day after Amelia arrived in Perryville, Ann and Ned drove over from Pine Hill for a visit. Lois treated them to a fancy lunch at Perryville's best eatery, The Carlisle Restaurant. At lunch, without Mallory present, Lois told them the news none of them wanted to hear. Lois is ill. Mallory doesn't know.

CHAPTER 16

THE PROFESSIONALS

FINN GALFORD CALLED his supplier, Craig Cutler, and his buddy Eddy Winger, as soon as he left the interrogation by Sheriff Highbrand. Finn gets all of his weed from a group of professional growers. He has connections with these men from his Army days. He stores the weed he deals at Eddy Winger's farm.

Cutler is an ex-Army Ranger. He knows every bit of usable terrain throughout Appalachia for growing marijuana. His outfit employs dozens of workers and uses drones to scan the grow sites.

Depending on the remoteness of the operation, he'll bring in box trucks and a group of usuals to do the wet trimming of a crop during the harvest. Eddy Winger is part of that large gang of usuals, made up mostly of ex-Army and ex-cons. There's decent money for skilled wet trimmers. On occasion, when Cutler's harvest is a cut and run, Winger will be brought in to do the dry trimming offsite.

It looked to Finn like the sheriff possibly stumbled into one of his supplier's grow operations on Dowd's Peak. It made sense. Old-timers who grazed sheep on hillsides a hundred years ago cleared large swaths of the forest from their mountaintops. Vacated pasture land is ideal as summer sites for the illegal grow industry.

Finn told Cutler that an anonymous blogger posted about wild cannabis growing at the top of Dowd's Peak. It created a lot of buzz in the Pine Hill area. Cutler confirmed what Finn suspected. The field is Cutler's operation. Cutler explained, "We've been using that two acres of land every summer for the last fourteen years."

Finn mentioned, "There was a timber clear cut about a mile away. That tipped off the sheriff. He put a camera up there. I saw your field, but there are wild plants growing all over the woods. I hadn't been up there since I was a kid."

Cutler said, "My drone picked up the Franklin Logging site. I was just trying to give the big crop a few more weeks. There's plenty of feral weed up on Dowd's because we've been there so many years. We're not particularly interested in that stuff."

Finn asked, "How'd you find Durbin's land fourteen years ago?"

Cutler responded, "Rather not say. Thanks, man, for the heads up on the sheriff."

Finn replied, "You bet!"

After Finn's conversation on Wednesday morning, Cutler dispatched two of his men to Dowd's Peak. They entered the mountain on state land, then made their way to the dense woods adjacent to the grow site. They fired a few rounds in the air to scare off three teenagers who were definitely not in the vicinity to hunt, but were lurking around the marijuana plants.

Wednesday afternoon, they watched a deputy sheriff walk from his truck to the cabin, then back to his truck and leave. They looked through the dilapidated cabin, but found nothing. They gave the all-clear for Cutler to come in with his team. From Thursday through mid-morning Friday the marijuana was cut and hauled away to be dry trimmed at Eddy Winger's farm.

CHAPTER 17
THE LAUGHINGSTOCK

DEVON AND MINT get to Dowd's Peak at about 10:30 a.m. It is a gloriously beautiful, pre-autumn morning on the mountain. Devon parks the cruiser across the top of Durbin's access road in plain sight of anyone approaching. The sight of the cruiser should keep the looky-loos away, who may be heading to "Cannabis Crest" on a mild Saturday morning. Devon thought Patty actually did him a favor.

Mint met Devon on her twenty-sixth birthday. He was at the Beasley County Courthouse for a deposition. The small staff at the courthouse threw a celebratory lunch for Mint. Devon's deposition wrapped up around noon. He and the attorney were invited to join everybody for cake and ice cream.

Mint had spotted Devon a few times around the building in the last couple of months. He was always in uniform, and she thought he was very handsome. She introduced herself to Devon after everyone sang "Happy Birthday." They traded the usual small talk during the lunch party. She explained her odd name: "My given name is Arminta. My younger sister couldn't say Rs." The next day, Mint called Devon at his office to thank him for celebrating her birthday with her.

Devon notices something is different as he exits the cruiser. The worn pathway into the woods is more heavily trampled. He leads Mint down the path toward the marijuana crop. From a ways off, he can tell it is all gone. Devon holds Mint back. He doesn't want to walk into the toxic herbicide if the feds have gotten there early. But he detects no chemical odor. There is no blue tinge on the ground, a sign of Paraquat. The feds have not been there.

Devon signals Mint to come ahead. She's surprised at the size of the grow operation. Devon can't believe this huge crop is gone. He tells Mint, "Deputy Cotten just removed the surveillance midweek. So, in the last two days, the entire crop was harvested."

Mint asks, "Who do you think did this?"

Devon's immediate thought turns to Finn Galford. Someone knows exactly what his sheriff's department is doing. He thinks there might actually be surveillance around the grow operation that he and Cotten had not spotted. So, he suggests to Mint, "Let's get out of here."

A million thoughts are swirling around in Devon's head. Was it Finn? He even wondered if that twenty-five-year-old narc Welton hired to meet with Finn was trustworthy. Devon knows he'll be a laughingstock to the feds and Milford. Welton will be livid!

Devon didn't want the day with Mint to be ruined, although his mood had drastically changed. She suggested they go back to her place. He thought it too risky. They weren't that far from the Ridgecrest Ski Runs. The guys at the lodge know him. He's in uniform, driving the cruiser. They'd just assume he's working on Saturday. He'll drop Mint at the coffee kiosk in the square, get a room for the day, and then she can come to his room. They can spend the afternoon together.

CHAPTER 18

THE FINAL TRAP

DEPUTY COTTEN IS waiting for Katy when she arrives at her apartment from the market Saturday afternoon. He beams when her car comes around the corner and parks. He approaches the driver's side door and opens it for her.

Katy steps out of the car. She asks, "Why are you here?" She wondered how long he'd been waiting for her. He came in his own truck. He's in civilian clothes. His hair is all slicked back.

Deputy Cotten explains, "You have to go and pick up the marijuana Finn Galford collected for your boyfriend."

Katy asks, "Now?"

Deputy Cotten replies, "No. Later."

Katy asks, "Will I be meeting Brian Hager again?"

Deputy Cotten quizzes Katy, "Why? Do you like Hager? Did you like pretending to be his girlfriend?" Katy doesn't say anything. Deputy Cotten grabs a grocery bag and follows Katy up her steps. As before, he comments that her ass looks good in her jeans.

Deputy Cotten sits himself down at Katy's kitchen table. "Is there any cold beer in the fridge?" She can smell booze on his breath. He reeks in so many ways. She pours him a glass of sweet tea. He says, "Thanks. No. You're not meeting Hager. You just go get the weed from Finn. The Finn Galford sting is over."

Deputy Cotten explains he will drop Katy just outside the trailer park. She isn't going to party at Finn's. She'll just grab the marijuana and leave. That is the setup. He lingers at the kitchen table as she puts some groceries away. He tells her, "I'll pick you up at nine o'clock. Sheriff Highbrand says you're done after tonight."

Katy replies, "Seriously?"

Cotten ignores her and says, "I like your hair like that. You should wear it like that tonight." Cotten gets up and goes toward Katy, cornering her in the kitchen. She turns her back to him and braces herself against the counter. A sensation of fight or flight shoots through her body as her reflexes prepare to fend off the deputy. Cotten bats her ponytail a couple of times, making it swing back and forth. He chuckles while he's doing that. Then his eyes focus on the cute butterfly tattoo on her neck. He touches it with his finger. He wants to ask if it's her only tattoo, but stops himself. He puts his empty glass in the sink and leaves the apartment, saying, "See ya later."

Cotten arrives back at Katy's place at 8:30 p.m. He bounds excitedly up the steps. He knocks. No answer. He knocks again. No answer. From the bottom of the steps, Cotten can see that the light's on in her bedroom. He waits next to his car, drinking from a can of beer.

Katy emerges right at nine o'clock, as planned. The ponytail that made her look like a high schooler is gone. Katy says, "My boyfriend Lou and I have some friends coming over."

Lou says, "Hey," to Deputy Cotten from the open door to Katy's apartment.

Deputy Cotten ignores Lou's greeting. He smashes his empty beer can on the ground with his boot. He says to Katy, "Get in the truck." Lou watches as Deputy Cotten speeds away with Katy.

CHAPTER 19

THE SHERIFF OF MAYHEM

SNEAKING MINT INTO the Ridgecrest Lodge worked out great. Late in the afternoon, Devon emerges from a dazed euphoria of liquor and lovemaking. Empty bottles from the room's mini-fridge are strewn over his side table. He turns on his phone to find seven missed calls from Patty. Something immediately hits him like a ton of bricks. He wonders if she'd found the condoms he'd forgotten in the trousers he threw over the chair when he was hurriedly forced to change from civilian clothes to his uniform. He knows the answer. Luckily, Mint had come prepared.

Mint rolls over and looks at Devon. She is lovely and amazing. He is not going to give this woman up. She grabs another condom from her side table. In Devon's mind, nothing matters anymore. He can't deal with the wife or the job. He turns his phone off again. He wants to disappear into this woman for as long as he can. He wants his life to change.

Devon makes his way back to Pine Hill around one a.m., having never called Patty to give his whereabouts. He knows better than to worry her. But the events of the day made Devon feel completely disengaged from his normal life. He plans to crash in the cabin when he gets home to avoid a nasty confrontation. But as he pulls in front of the cabin, he can see lights flashing red and blue in front of his house up on the hill.

Freddy Hoover had reached Devon an hour earlier. Patty called both deputies that night, looking for her husband. Freddy was on call. Deputy Cotten never got back to her.

As Devon drives up the hill, he sees Freddy sitting with Patty on the front porch. Devon's in no mood for the requisite disapproval from his goody-two-shoes deputy whose father is preacher at the Pine Hill Methodist Church.

From his driver's side window, Devon says to his wife, "We'll talk tomorrow!" Patty doesn't say anything in front of Freddy. Devon asks Freddy to follow him back down the hill. Parked outside the cabin, Devon apologizes, "Sorry for the late night. You didn't need you to sit with my wife until I got here." Then Devon launches into his big sob story about the harvested crop.

Freddy has never liked Devon and hates serving under him. He had voted for Angus Ungebuhler to remain as sheriff. Freddy knew Devon would be bad for the county. He interrupts Devon's rambling diatribe about the lost marijuana bust and informs his boss, "The department has far bigger problems than Dowd's. I just took a call from the sheriff's office in Beasley. Cotten raped your C.I. tonight."

CHAPTER 20
SCORCHED EARTH

"THE INDICTMENT CHARGES rape, battery, kidnapping, sexual abuse, assault, and abuse of process," says Samuel Farraday in his opening statement. Farraday approaches the jury box as he describes, to a packed courtroom, the events leading up to the rape trial of Wally Cotten that he's prosecuting.

Farraday continues, "Ladies and gentlemen, on the night in question, Wallace Cotten picked Kate Legonick up from her apartment in Sizemore at 9 p.m. Ms. Legonick was told earlier that day that she was to perform a planned errand for the sheriff's department in the town of Arlodale. Farraday points to Devon, who is seated behind Wally Cotten, and explains, "Sheriff Devon Highbrand confirmed in his deposition that Ms. Legonick was completing her role as part of a sting operation. You will also hear directly from Sheriff Highbrand that Ms. Legonick was to be released from her role as his confidential informant after the completion of her errand that night."

Interrupting Farraday's delivery, someone in the courtroom yells out an obscenity-laced accusation directed at Devon and

Cotten regarding the sting operation. Judge Herbert Crawford admonishes the unruly disrupter with a warning of immediate expulsion, should there be another outburst. After the courtroom settles down Judge Crawford says to Farraday, "You may continue."

Farraday says, "Thank you, Your Honor!" To the jury he states: "Instead of taking Ms. Legonick to the town of Arlodale to complete her planned errand, Deputy Cotten kidnapped Ms. Legonick and engaged the young woman in a terrifying drive, speeding dangerously through hairpin turns all the way to the town of Flintville, where the assault happened!"

Cotten's attorney rises to address Judge Crawford and asks for a sidebar. Devon takes the opportunity to turn around to scan the packed courtroom. He's curious as to whether Mint decided to watch some of the trial. Patty, who's seated next to Devon, knows exactly what he's doing. She turns to look also, hoping for a first sighting of the homewrecker.

Patty's refusing to grant Devon a divorce. She feels she'll never have to with the trouble he's in. She lives in their dream home on the hill. Devon resides in the drafty cabin, running to Opal's every morning for a shower and breakfast. Devon convinced Patty that they had to put the sixty acres they owned into the name of their eldest son, Alan, or risk losing it in civil litigation.

Earlier that morning, Mint watched from her office window as her handsome, uniformed boyfriend entered the Beasley County Courthouse, hand in hand with his wife. She knows the public display of affection between Devon and Patty is just for show. But she hates the sight.

Devon's public persona as that of a devoted family man and faithful public servant is paramount right now. Katy is also accusing Devon of negligent training and violation of retention supervision, among other things. The scandal appeared in the local papers and was picked up by a national news outlet two days after Cotten was arrested.

"… the FBI received several complaints alleging inappropriate conduct by a sheriff's deputy at the department. Some of the same conduct appears to have been occurring for years, while under the supervision of the currently serving sheriff. Specifics of the investigation are not being released. The FBI is advising that federal implications may be revealed."

Patty hates sitting in the courtroom next to her cheating husband and behind the rapist's defense table. She woke up that morning to a blog posted by General Sherman's Ghost which read, "Big Badge didn't care if Little Badge had sex with underage girls, as long as he took it out of his county." They argued all the way to Perryville about how she can't show her face around Pine Hill anymore. Patty swore she wouldn't attend another day of the trial after this opening day. Devon said the blog was ridiculous.

After scouring the courtroom for Mint, Patty sizes up Katy Legonick. Katy must have felt Patty staring. She turns from her seat at the prosecutor's table to make eye contact. Patty immediately diverts her eyes. Patty was fired from her social work job by the county commission as soon as it came out that Devon gained leverage over Katy based on his wife's reporting. The commission had already received a letter from Livia Bangertt's probation officer alleging Patty stole an ivory cameo necklace that was on Livia's coffee table.

Devon knows the remainder of his term as sheriff is scorched earth. The job was no longer a stepping stone to something grander. Not only is Deputy Cotten gone, but his ally in the prosecutor's office is gone, too. George Lee Welton III was forced to resign as county prosecutor four months after the Cotten arrest.

Somehow, Welton escaped prosecution. It took a challenge to his law license to reveal his criminal behavior. Welton was merely stripped of his license to practice law for three years.

Not only had Betty Braedon come forward about what Welton did to her, another woman detailed the depraved encounter she had with Welton inside the county prosecutor's office. In that instance, Welton's girlfriend from eighteen years back, Thelma Riddle, was propositioned by Welton at a yard sale. Thelma is newly married to Thurson "Sonny" Riddle.

Sonny Riddle is a respected landowner in Pine Hill. He owns one hundred and forty-seven acres with a green apple orchard and currant bushes, and he raises goats. He sells jams and goat milk products each year at the Ungebuhler farmstand. Thelma is Sonny's second wife.

At the time Welton dated Thelma, he was twenty-seven and she was nineteen. On two different nights, Welton secretly recorded video of them having sex in the back room at the sheriff's department. He told Thelma he planned to share the videos with Sonny unless she came to his office the following week. She doubted Welton had videos of her from when he served as deputy sheriff. But since he put her on the spot at a public outing in front of her friends, she quietly agreed to meet with him.

Thelma returned home and told Sonny what Welton said. They immediately contacted the state police. Since Betty Braedon had already come forward about what Welton did to her, the FBI was brought in on the matter. Special Agent Tim Ridgely asked Thelma if she would be comfortable wearing a wire at her meeting with Welton. Thelma agreed.

When Thelma arrived at the prosecutor's office, she could hear the blaring audio of their sexual encounter. Welton was viewing the videos. He spun the computer around to show Thelma. Welton said he would delete everything if she stripped naked in his office. When she refused, Welton stood up from behind his desk, his privates exposed. He came close to Thelma asking her to touch and kiss his penis. He demanded oral sex in exchange for the videos. The only thing Thelma said to Welton during the encounter was, "Where are your pants?" Then she left the office.

Welton was interviewed by S.A. Ridgely the following day. Welton said he didn't know she was wearing a wire, and admitted it was stupid to ask her to kiss his penis.

CHAPTER 21
POA

WHILE OPAL NEVER liked Patty, she approves of Mint. Opal thinks Mint is the kind of beauty Devon should have married in the first place. And now that Devon is spending his free time in Perryville, he can really ingratiate himself to Lois, who is terminally ill. Opal refuses to go to Perryville to help Lois and Mallory. But she is always curious as to her sister's stage of decline.

Devon stopped by Lois's almost daily in the weeks leading up to her death. He assured Mallory he'd take care of her when her mother died. Devon was advised by Lois that Pinion Echo Bank and Trust will be Mallory's trustee for her trust fund and that her last will and testament is unchanged. All of her assets go into The Revocable Trust of Lois Fleetwood, for the sole benefit of Mallory. Devon and his brother remain as her executors. Opal was not happy to learn from Devon that she wasn't in her sister's will.

Instead of Lois receiving hospice care in Perryville in her final days, Devon took Lois to a facility run by his buddy in Sizemore. This is what Opal wanted, not what Mallory wanted or expected.

Mallory had been told that Lois would remain in Perryville until she died. Opal wanted a final look at her dying sister.

Mallory was left alone for the first time in her life. Not knowing what was happening to her mother, she started cutting herself on her stomach. Once she was badly bleeding, Mallory knew enough to dial 911. She was taken to a psychiatric hospital two hours north of Perryville for evaluation. During that week of involuntary commitment she was counseled and put on a combination of antidepressants and other drugs which worsened her confusion.

Ann and Ned brought Mallory from the psychiatric hospital to Pine Hill to stay with them when she was released. Mallory was a mess, as the drugs she was prescribed were not good for her mental disabilities. She was not cutting herself, but she didn't want to eat anything. Mallory claimed she was itchy and she would pick at her skin.

The Boones took her to Sizemore to see Lois just before she died. Lois had been unresponsive to Opal's chatter. But in her final moments she rallied for Mallory. Lois took Mallory's face in her hands and told her sobbing daughter, "Be brave and live a full, happy life."

On the day Lois died, Patty was seen going into the Fleetwood residence in Perryville. Her presence was noticed by one of Lois's neighbors, who had just been informed that Lois had passed. The cottage was a mess, with Lois's soiled bedding and clothing scattered about, and old dirty dishes in the sink. Patty could have helped tidy up the place. Instead, she rummaged through every drawer and cabinet, leaving the place looking more ransacked. Patty searched until she found the contract for her $50,000 loan. She left with the contract and over two hundred dollars in cash from Lois's nightstand.

Mallory told Ann and Ned she wanted to go back to her own home the day after her mom died. She missed the personal things that gave her comfort. She missed her music and her computer games and her bedroom. Mallory promised Ann she wouldn't harm herself.

Devon told the Boones he'd drive Mallory home and make sure she was comfortably settled. He also promised Ann he'd see to it that Mallory got her medications. He'd arrange for a nurse to come see her every day. Devon was dying to be with Mint, and he had some important business to take care of with Mallory.

It would be some time before Devon could go to any bank, as executor of Lois Fleetwood's estate. So, he downloaded a two-page power of attorney document from the website, "Legal Documents For Dummies." It will give Devon and Opal the right to act as agents for Mallory. They'll have access to Mallory's personal bank account.

On the drive from Pine Hill to Perryville, Devon scolded Mallory for her behavior. He explained to her, "You better do what I say from now on, or I'll take you back to the psych ward."

They stopped at a tiny luncheonette on the outskirts of town. After getting Mallory to eat a few fries, Devon announced, "I'm going to be your lawful POA." Devon surmised that a mysterious legal-sounding designation would seem serious to someone with Mallory's cognitive challenges. He felt fortunate that Lois never had Mallory declared legally incompetent. Devon advised, "I have urgent documents for you to sign." Mallory signed everything.

Devon settled Mallory into her torn-apart cottage, then went to the business office at the Terrace Residences looking for a notary public. An older woman named Gail Bowers introduced herself as the business manager for the complex. She's a notary. Gail had gotten to know Lois and Mallory quite well. She cares a great deal about what is to become of Mallory, now that Lois is gone.

Gail looked at the document Devon presented to be notarized. She thought it highly suspect that this man had Mallory sign a power of attorney document on the very day after Lois died. It was clearly something he just grabbed off the internet. Gail believed if Lois wanted Devon Highbrand and his mother to act as Mallory's attorneys-in-fact, she would have set this up some time ago. Gail pointed out to Devon, "Mallory already signed the power of attorney document. She'll need to sign in the presence of a notary for this to be legal."

Devon responded, "I completely understand. We'll do it another day, when Mallory can come in person."

Gail asked, "How is Mallory? Please tell her if she needs anything to call me. I'm sorry for your loss!"

Devon thanked Gail for her condolences and left the business office. He was furious. He was in no mood for some principled notary. He picked Mint up and they hurried back to his office in Sizemore. The sheriff department's notary, Lisa, will do what she is told.

As Lois wrapped up her affairs in the weeks before her death, she sold her rustic mountain condo near the ski runs. Lois advised Devon to put the profits from the real estate sale into her personal savings account, so the money will go directly into the trust fund.

A $173,000 settlement check for the mountain condo, made out jointly to co-owners Lois Fleetwood and Mallory Fleetwood, arrived at their residence while Lois was at the Sizemore hospice. Per Devon's instructions, Mallory endorsed the check. It was deposited it into Mallory's personal checking account, making those funds available to Opal and Devon.

CHAPTER 22
"BYE BYE TRUST FUND"

AMELIA WOULD HAVE two, and only two conversations with Opal after Lois died. Opal said something to Amelia on the first call that was really disturbing. The call began with Amelia expressing her sympathies, "I'm so sorry, Aunt Opal, for your loss."

Opal replied, "Lois is being cremated and there isn't going to be a funeral." Then Opal said, "Mallory has no reason to live. She has no brothers." There was a pause because clearly, Amelia was taken aback by Opal's comment. During the pause, Opal said, "Okay. Take care of yourself." She quickly hung up. Amelia always thought Opal to be a bit dumb and kooky. But that was just weird.

Amelia wrote a lovely obituary for Lois. It ran in two of the D.C. papers, the *Sizemore Gazette* and the little *Perryville Chronicle*. Two days after the obituary appeared in the *Sizemore Gazette*, Leeland Culp called Devon. Mr. Culp suggested they meet, soon, at his office. He's anxious to arrange Lois Fleetwood's trust fund, which his bank will be handling for Mallory.

Devon discussed with Opal, multiple times, during their daily breakfasts, how he wants to get rid of Mallory's trust fund. One morning, it is finally settled in his mind: "No one will question what I do with Lois's estate. I'm her executor. I'm a sheriff."

Opal wants to know, "What have you told Mint?"

Devon responds, "Nothing. She doesn't know anything about Lois. Nobody in Beasley County knows what Lois was worth. If I get rid of the trust, you and I will be in charge of all the money. We'll control what Mallory gets."

Mother and son shared the same thought: *Why should Mallory get all of the money when we can be spending it?*

They discuss keeping Randolph out of their plans. Opal's concerned he'll spill the beans to Janice. Devon absolutely agrees. Randolph is to know nothing about any of this. Devon and Opal discuss how much time they'll have to show financial support for Mallory without anyone becoming suspicious that there isn't actually a trust fund.

When Devon arrives at Pinion Echo Bank and Trust, Leeland Culp has the prepared documents needed to implement the trust fund. Devon gets his first look at the revised trust document. Sure enough, he and Randolph are no longer the trustees. He will have zero access to Lois's money if it all goes into the trust fund. Mr. Culp's name is on the amended and restated trust agreement, which cites Pinion Echo Bank and Trust as the trust fund's sole trustee. It was signed by Lois, dated, and notarized prior to her move to Perryville, nearly two years before her death. Devon inquires, "I see the date of your signature was over two years ago. Was that the last time you saw my aunt?"

Mr. Culp answers, "I met with Mrs. Fleetwood twice. We had an initial meeting about the bank becoming her trustee. And, then we met again after the trust document was written for both parties to sign. Then, I spoke to her about a year ago. I knew she was ill at that time."

Devon informs Mr. Culp that unfortunately, many changes had taken place in Mrs. Fleetwood's life in the last year. He spends a good five minutes explaining that Lois had a long and expensive illness. Devon says, "What money was left over, Lois decided should just go into her daughter's name." Devon states the bottom line to Mr. Culp: "There is no money to fund a trust."

Devon leaves the meeting with Culp, relieved and surprised that this man didn't ask any questions. Devon had polished and buffed his black shoes and shined his brass badge before going to the bank that day. The uniform still packs a great deal of clout, and perceived integrity, apparently.

Devon waited for several days after the meeting with Culp for any blowback, half expecting a call from the bank's legal department. But no call ever came. The biggest hurdle in his plan to destroy Lois's trust, Leeland Culp, is in the rearview mirror.

Devon went on to submit the rest of what he had to provide to Beasley County to close the Fleetwood estate. The value of the estate appraisal Devon submits is $94,718. Because the amount is under $100,000, no probate court is triggered.

Beasley County Clerk, Roni Wagner, types on the appraisal document what the will lawfully stipulates. Lois's sole beneficiary is "The Revocable Trust of Lois Fleetwood." Before Ms. Wagner can stamp and record the official document, Devon crosses out "The Revocable Trust of Lois Fleetwood." Underneath in the beneficiary column, he handwrites in "Mallory Fleetwood, daughter."

Ms. Wagner doesn't question why the executor of the estate changed the beneficiary from the decedent's last will and testament. Why would she? This charming sheriff is dating her good friend, Mint, who works across the hall.

Devon watches as Roni Wagner stamps the document. An electrical flash crosses from left to right in Devon's chest cavity. His conscience correctly recognizes the flash as a pang of guilt. His brain immediately dismisses that notion and identifies the sensation as gas from Opal's fried scrapple breakfast. He takes in a couple of deep breaths to steady himself. It's official. All that Lois Fleetwood technically owes to her new and improved beneficiary, Mallory Fleetwood, is $94,718. Everything Lois Fleetwood planned over the last fifty years to ensure her impaired daughter's secure financial future is destroyed. Devon mutters under his breath, "Bye, bye trust fund."

Devon and Opal are all set. They're in control of over $2 Million. They now need to get rid of the Mallory problem.

CHAPTER 23

THE MERCEDES

ALL IN ALL, two grand juries delivered fifty-seven indictments against Deputy Wally Cotten, including sex with an incarcerated woman and sex crimes against girls as young as fifteen years old. But because of his good ol' boy status in an environment with mostly good ol' boys in charge, Cotten was able to plead down to just one criminal count. For the rape of Katy Legonick, he got ten-to-twenty years.

The county coughed up a substantial settlement to Katy for Sheriff Highbrand's role in the shifty marijuana sting. And because the national press had made a huge story out of the crimes and ineptitude by county law enforcement, citizens would get to vote, in the next election, on whether sheriff would continue to be an elected position. The county commission wouldn't get to choose the deputies either. There'd be a more robust determination process outside of county cronyism. Early polling suggests it isn't such a good idea to elect a person with zero training and experience to be the top cop.

Patty is the only person Devon, and, reluctantly, Opal, trust to keep her mouth shut about Mallory's trust fund being destroyed. If she doesn't, she'll lose everything. For her silence, Devon bought Patty a brand-new Mercedes. He also gave her $15,000 to remodel the drafty cabin. Janice overheard Patty telling two women at the post office that plumbing had just gone in and the cabinets were coming all the way from a company in Richmond. To purchase his complete estrangement from her, Devon decided to start paying Patty $1,000 a month. On the memo line on the $1,000 checks Patty receives out of Mallory's checking account, Devon writes: "Therapist." Devon has Mallory sign all the checks.

Because he's being so generous with Lois's fortune, Patty is granting Devon a divorce, on one condition. He can't move in with Mint unless he is going to marry her. Patty has some cockamamy idea that if Devon leaves her for a woman he intends to marry, it will be less humiliating.

Devon and Patty spare no expense for a lavish wedding on Opal's farm for their eldest daughter Megan. Megan never became a Miss America contestant, but a dental hygienist. She fell in love with an oil field roughneck from Louisiana, whom she met on a cruise she took with her girlfriends after high school.

Devon is ecstatic on Megan's wedding day. Not for his daughter's nuptials, because he doesn't care much for the roughneck. But because Patty signed the divorce papers the night before. As soon as the kids dance their last dance, he's off to see Mint as a free man. He's hatched a plan to stay in Perryville, without technically residing with Mint, and he can't wait to get that ball rolling.

CHAPTER 24

UNSPEAKABLE PAYNE

ANN BOONE'S FATHER, Eugene Sennett, and Opal rarely speak. They will only if someone dies, or they arrive at church at the same time, and greeting each other is unavoidable. Eugene hated Fletcher due to something Fletcher did involving Eugene and Opal's older brother Payne. Because of it, Eugene and Opal have been estranged for decades.

Eugene and Payne were as close as brothers could be. One summer, right after Opal and Fletcher were married, Fletcher and Payne went hunting with Henry and Estes Durbin. The four of them camped out in Durbin's cabin on Dowd's Peak. Henry and Estes left after two nights. But Payne and Fletcher decided to stay another day, to see if they could bag a big buck. They both got drunk that third night. When Fletcher woke up the following day around noon, Payne was nowhere to be found. Fletcher searched the forest for about an hour. As he was about to head down the mountain to get help, he found Payne collapsed in the driver's seat of his old truck. He was dead.

Fletcher got them back down the mountain and to a doctor's

office. Payne had multiple rattlesnake bites to his feet. Fletcher presumed he had gone out of the cabin to take a leak in the middle of the night. After being bitten, Payne must have thought to try to get himself down the mountain in Fletcher's truck. The key, which would normally be left in the ignition, wasn't there. The coroner could tell that asphyxiation was the actual cause of death. Payne had a violent reaction to the amount of venom he was exposed to, combined with intoxication, and suffered a totally constricted airway from vomiting.

Payne's horrible death was an unfortunate tragedy. But Fletcher told everyone in town that Payne ended up dead because he was a lightweight who couldn't hold his liquor. Eugene and his parents always wondered about Fletcher's story, and why the key wasn't in the truck. Did Payne try to wake up Fletcher for help? Was Fletcher the one who was dead drunk? Eugene, in particular out of Opal's siblings, never forgave Fletcher for smearing his dead brother's name. Some old wounds never heal.

Eugene called Opal to ask the whereabouts of Lois's ashes. Ann told him Mallory doesn't have the remains. He has an extra plot at the Arlodale Cemetery, next to their brother Payne, that he wants to offer to Mallory. He thinks it will be nice, when Mallory dies someday, that Lois and Mallory could lie in peace together, with their ashes interred in the same cemetery plot. Eugene reminded Opal that Lois always said she wanted to be near Payne when she died, because she adored her brother so much. Opal said she has the ashes, but she'll have to ask Devon about all of that.

CHAPTER 25

THE APARTMENT

THE DAY AFTER Megan's big wedding, Devon met with a landlord in Perryville about a two-bedroom apartment near the small town's shops. His plan is to rent the apartment with Mallory's money, and move there. This will satisfy his arrangement with Patty, which is to not live with Mint until they're engaged.

He'll move Mallory into the apartment with him. He can give Mallory her pills and fire the nurse to save some money. He'll instruct Mallory to tell Ann and Amelia that Devon found her a cute place much cheaper than the cottage.

Devon transferred for himself a $102,000 money market account balance from a joint account Lois shared with Mallory, and deposited the money into Mallory's checking account. He plunked down $60,000 from that allotment to Harold Reinhardt of Reinhardt Construction, to build a paved bridge over the creek on his sixty acres. Patty kept complaining that the water would get too high for her to cross the creek in her new Mercedes.

Devon began paying himself a stipend of $3,000 a month because the sheriff's salary is ending, and Patty's alimony and child support suck up all of his military pension. Combining the money market account with the profit from the mountain condo, and the roughly $29,000 that was in Mallory's checking account from before Lois died, Devon and Opal are rapidly blowing through a slush fund of a little over $300,000. Devon told his mother she should withdraw enough money from Mallory's checking account to cover all of her expenses for the coming year.

When Opal explains Eugene's plans for Lois's ashes, Devon instructs his mother, "Don't talk to him anymore. You'll keep the ashes." As far as Devon is concerned, Opal's possession of the remains can still be useful in keeping Mallory under control. Opal threatened to throw Lois's ashes in Devon's creek at one point. That seemed to keep Mallory quiet.

CHAPTER 26
FENTANYL

ON A THURSDAY afternoon, from her apartment in downtown Perryville, Mallory is on her landline to Gail Bowers. That same afternoon, in downtown Sizemore, a care-free Devon is enjoying a Christmas celebration with his colleagues. He's hanging all over Mint and getting sloshed on spiked eggnog. His term as sheriff is over in a couple weeks. The party is also a gathering to congratulate Freddy Hoover who will become the next sheriff.

It had been four months since Devon moved Mallory into the apartment in downtown Perryville. At first, it had been nice for Mallory. She told Ann and Amelia she liked walking to the little shops by herself. Devon would make food for Mallory, like soup, or bring her takeout. Devon and Mint had even taken her out to dinner with them once.

But Mallory is ill all the time. She tells Gail on the phone, she's sick from the pills Devon is giving her every morning, and asks Gail to take her to the doctor. Gail hadn't seen Mallory since Devon moved her away from the Terrace Residences. When Gail picked up Mallory, she was alarmed. Mallory's very skinny. She has lesions on her face and arms. To Gail, she looks like an AIDS sufferer. Gail drove her immediately to the John R. Clyburn Clinic in downtown Perryville.

Inside the clinic, in what Mallory perceives is a safe space, she pours her heart out to a doctor, through tears. Mallory attributes her weight loss to constant vomiting. "I'm always nauseated," she says.

The doctor looks down at her chart to see she weighs 102 pounds on a 5'7" frame. Mallory tells the doctor her POA is mean to her. She says he'll threaten her if she doesn't want to take her pills every morning. So she takes them. Then when he leaves, she will try to throw up.

Gail interrupts Mallory to tell the doctor, "The POA Mallory is talking about is Mallory's cousin Devon Highbrand. He also acts as her power of attorney."

Mallory says, "I don't know what to do, but I can't go on like this. So, I called Gail."

A nurse draws blood from Mallory. Six hours later the test confirms there is fentanyl in Mallory's system along with the psychiatric drugs. Mallory is referred to a social worker, who begins an adult protective services case against Devon Highbrand.

Gail takes Mallory home after spending all evening at the clinic. She stays with her through the night. Devon comes in the morning to give Mallory her cocktail of pills, and finds Gail with Mallory.

At first, Devon had no idea who Gail was, then remembers she is the obnoxious notary at the Terrace Residences. Gail hands him papers acknowledging the APS complaint. She advises Devon that Mallory will be staying in the apartment while the APS social worker pursues her case. He is to live elsewhere. Gail tells Devon not to enter the premises again, and informs him she'll be helping Mallory file for a restraining order.

Devon argues with Gail. He accuses her of meddling where she doesn't belong. He tells her she has no idea what Mallory is like, and that Mallory is a liar. He insists he has taken care of Mallory since her mother died. He's done everything for her. Mallory is just very ungrateful and lazy. Devon warns Gail she doesn't know who she's dealing with.

After he leaves, Mallory tells Gail she isn't a liar, something Gail already knows. Gail asks Mallory why she didn't tell someone about all of this before now. Mallory says, "I don't want to worry anyone." Gail asks, "What about your relatives in Pine Hill?" Mallory gives her the number for Ann Boone.

By midday, Mallory is feeling a little better without the morning medications. As instructed, Gail plans to return Mallory to the clinic to be evaluated for new prescriptions to ease her off of the addictive garbage she had been taking. But before that, Gail wants to know if Mallory is strong enough to go to her bank. She wants Mallory to get a printout of her checking account statement. Mallory says, "I'm able to go to the bank."

CHAPTER 27

"WHEN THE MONEY'S GONE ..."

THE FRONT PAGE story in the Perryville newspaper states,

"Commissioner arrested for unlawful entry to Perryville Regional Airport. Beasley County Commissioner, Calvin Griffin, age 56, broke into the airport terminal last night. Griffin confiscated an airport computer and downloaded computer files he didn't have authorization to access, before returning the computer to the terminal. He is facing five misdemeanors for trespassing and theft of airport property."

Amelia's stuck in a Midwestern airport hotel for a second night. Her connecting flight on a ten-passenger jet into the tiny Perryville Regional Airport was canceled. The TSA has to assess the damage done by Calvin Griffin before resuming operations.

It's just days before Christmas. Amelia's going to Perryville to bring Mallory back to San Diego for the Christmas holiday. As she lay awake, Amelia wondered why her Aunt Lois had to move to a place that took at least two days to get to from anywhere in the US. She also wondered why Calvin Griffin wasn't behind bars in federal lockup for breaking into an airport terminal and stealing computer files. Sadly, she knows that answer. He's a white good ol' boy in Appalachia!

The day after Gail Bowers made an urgent call to Ann Boone on Mallory's behalf, Amelia had her second and final phone conversation with Opal. It was even more disturbing than the first call when Opal said, "Mallory has no reason to live. She has no brothers."

Opal was furious with Mallory for accusing Devon of abuse. She told Amelia, "She can't say things like that about Devon. Devon is washing his hands of her. And when the money's gone, it's gone."

Amelia asked Opal what she meant by "And when the money's gone, it's gone." Amelia demanded to know who managed Mallory's trust fund. That's when Opal told Amelia, "There isn't one."

Amelia didn't sleep for three nights after her call with Opal. She can't believe there isn't a trust fund for Mallory. Where did all of Lois's money go? In her mind, she kept replaying the comment, "And when the money's gone, it's gone."

Amelia's in direct contact with Gail Bowers. She spent hours on the phone with her trying to figure things out. Gail was so relieved to speak to someone who can help out Mallory.

A year before Lois died, she gave Gail a list of financial institutions where her assets were distributed. Lois asked Gail to hold the list for safekeeping. Gail sent that list to Amelia. Also included in the package was Mallory's checking account statement, Mallory's clinic paperwork, and an address book. In Lois's old address book was the name, phone number, and date of payment to attorney Glenda Thompson Haas. Beneath Glenda's name, Lois had written "Trust Fund."

Amelia scheduled a meeting with attorney Glenda Thompson Haas on the morning she arrived in Perryville. Ms. Haas had forwarded to Amelia the "Amended and Restated Trust Agreement," naming Pinion Echo Bank and Trust as sole trustee of Mallory's trust fund. That document gave Amelia the name of Leeland Culp, whose signature is on the trust papers.

Culp confirmed to Amelia what Opal said. There is no trust fund at his bank. He said, "I met with Sheriff Highbrand after Mrs. Fleetwood died. The sheriff explained to me there was no money for a trust fund." Amelia advised Culp not to speak to Devon again.

Amelia instructed Gail Bowers to get Mallory ready to travel. No one was to know Amelia was coming to Perryville. She worried what the Highbrands might do if they knew. Other than Gail and Mallory, only Ann was alerted to Amelia's plans. Ann would meet Amelia, Mallory, and Gail at Glenda's office.

At the meeting, Amelia asked Glenda, "Why didn't Lois revise her last will and testament to remove Devon and Randolph as executors of her estate?"

Glenda said, "Regrettably, I advised Lois that it wasn't really necessary. I looked at the will. Your aunt's will and trust documents couldn't have been more clearly articulated. She did everything correctly in making those end of life decisions. Executors are required to follow the instructions in a will. It didn't occur to me Lois's lawful dictates would be undermined. Certainly not by someone in law enforcement."

Amelia replied, "Unfortunately, that is not the case."

Mallory signed a document at Glenda's office revoking Devon and Opal as her attorneys-in-fact. After the meeting, Glenda filed a probate petition at the Beasley County Commission which read, "Motion to Remove Devon Highbrand and Randolph Highbrand as Fiduciaries for the Lois Fleetwood Estate."

It is clear to Amelia that Devon funneled Lois's assets into Mallory's checking account for his own personal use and lied about Lois's wealth. And that's not to mention what Gail, Ann and Amelia all suspect: Devon was trying to kill Mallory with fentanyl!

CHAPTER 28

ASHES TO ASHES

"Bob" Merson can't believe his good luck. A day after New Year's, he's hired by Devon and handed a $5,000 retainer check, which he cashes immediately. Merson's scheduled to meet with both Devon and Randolph the following week. Merson knows this will be the first time the men have been together since their teenage years, except for Fletcher's funeral. They're bringing their wives, or in Devon's case, his ex-wife, and their mother.

Patty is seeing red. Devon just broke the news to her that her $1,000 monthly payment is ending. Patty screams at Devon, "How could you be stupid enough to let something happen to our financial windfall? All you had to do was be nice to Mallory!" Patty berates Devon for being all consumed with his tramp, Mint! She tells him, "I'm not giving up my Mercedes."

"This is the real world," exclaims Mallory, on one of her outings around San Diego with Amelia. She's so happy to be out of her dreary, isolated life and experiencing the beautiful California weather. They had a lovely Christmas together and celebrated New Year's Eve at a beachfront resort. Mallory didn't want to return to Perryville after her

Christmas holiday, and Amelia was glad that was Mallory's decision. There was no way she was returning Mallory to Appalachia.

Amelia informed Mallory of Eugene's wish to honor Lois with a lovely spot in the Arlodale Cemetery. Mallory picked out a beautiful headstone to be placed at the gravesite. She refers to her Aunt Opal as a witch. Mallory told Amelia, "I never want to talk to Opal again." So, Amelia helped Mallory write a letter to Opal, asking that she turn over Lois's ashes to Eugene and Ann.

Randolph stopped by Opal's at three p.m. one afternoon, ready to sit down to his mom's home cooking. Janice had taken their youngest to a birthday party. Randolph was on his own for supper. He opened Opal's back door, expecting to smell something delicious frying. Instead, Randolph found his mother on her sun porch, visibly upset. There was no food on the table and nothing on the stove. She hadn't prepared anything for him to eat!

Opal showed Randolph the letter from Mallory, which requested she relinquish Lois's ashes to Ann and Eugene. Opal tells Randolph, "I thought I was keeping Lois's ashes. Devon told me not to have any contact with Eugene. I don't know what to do."

Starving and furious, Randolph dusts off his good ol' boy hatefulness and pays Ann a visit. Ann hears a pounding on her front door. As she walks into the living room, she sees Randolph on her porch. She glances at Ned who'd been startled awake from dozing in his recliner. As she opens the door, Randolph smells the aroma of supper food coming from Ann's kitchen. It wafts into the freezing afternoon air and hits him directly in the face. It smells to Randolph like lasagna is baking or maybe sausages and peppers simmering in an Italian sauce. Then he realizes it's probably Italian stuffed peppers, his favorite!

After his moment of epicurean distraction Randolph begins yelling at Ann, "Those ashes can sit on a shelf for fifty years if I want, because I am executor of Lois's estate. The ashes belong to the estate. If you or Eugene come near my mother to get those ashes, I'll have you both arrested!"

Ann gets Amelia on speaker phone after Randolph's psychotic display of aggression. Ned confirms he had witnessed it, too. Amelia apologizes for putting them in that position with the disgusting Highbrands. She doesn't want to wait a minute longer to get Lois's ashes away from Opal. Amelia hangs up with Ann and Ned and calls Cantwell & Cantwell.

Cantwell & Cantwell is the funeral home that handled Lois's cremation. Amelia reaches Silas Cantwell. She's been speaking with Silas about providing the headstone that Mallory ordered for the gravesite. Amelia asks Silas to send her the funeral home's paperwork on Lois Fleetwood. He immediately emails the "Disposition of Cremated Remains" document signed by Lois two years before she died. It states her remains are to be given to her daughter Mallory.

Amelia asks Silas, "Why is it that Opal Highbrand has possession of Mrs. Fleetwood's ashes?"

Silas couldn't say. He replies to her inquiry, "Ms. Etchison, I can't find any documentation for your aunt's remains ever leaving this mortuary."

Amelia knows what happened. Devon flashed the sheriff's badge and took the ashes shortly after Lois died. She states in no uncertain terms to Silas, "I would strongly suggest you go this afternoon and retrieve the cremated remains of Lois Fleetwood from her sister, or there will be a lawsuit on your desk in the morning." Amelia demands an update later the same evening.

Cantwell & Cantwell is the only funeral business for the region. Father and son Silas Cantwell and Kenneth Cantwell are the owners. Perryville is the location for their mortuary and crematory. Then they have tiny chapel-type funeral parlors in places like Pine Hill. The Pine Hill funeral parlor only has staff present if a local viewing is arranged.

Silas decides he has no choice but to dispatch Bud Wright. Bud Wright lives in Arlodale. He is the favorite gravedigger of all Cantwell & Cantwell gravediggers. Bud is reliable, rain or shine. In the extreme winter months, he has never complained when forced to excavate the frozen ground.

Determined to keep Amelia in the loop, Silas phones Amelia to say, "Opal Highbrand has been contacted. Mrs. Highbrand was informed Bud Wright will collect the ashes later this evening."

Amelia replies jokingly, "Isn't Bud an odd name for an undertaker?"

Amelia thinks the whole ordeal can't get any stranger, until Silas says, "Bud is actually the Arlodale Cemetery gravedigger. He'll be taking Mrs. Fleetwood's ashes home with him tonight."

Amelia wants to sue Cantwell & Cantwell for even subjecting her to that last sentence. She lets Silas know the arrangement is completely unacceptable.

Silas assures Amelia, "Bud is the most trustworthy person I know. Early tomorrow morning, Bud will bring the ashes to the Cantwell & Cantwell Mortuary in Perryville. I'll make sure everything is fine when Bud is handed the ashes later tonight."

Silas offers Amelia the most beautiful and expensive burial box they have in stock for Mrs. Fleetwood's interment underground. He reassures Amelia he will personally transport Mrs. Fleetwood's remains to the Arlodale Cemetery whenever the day is chosen for her burial. And he'll provide beautiful flowers for her grave for a year, which Bud will switch out twice a month.

Amelia knows this is a done deal. She figures her Aunt Lois, wherever she is, is having a good laugh about spending the night with Bud. Later that night, Amelia receives word from Silas: "Bud picked up the ashes and everything is fine. The crematory box is still sealed, so there was no tampering of any sort."

Amelia's satisfied with Silas's efforts, but she's angry. Opal kept Lois's cremated remains from Mallory. Yet she couldn't be bothered to put the ashes in a tasteful vessel as a tribute to her sister. Instead, all this time, Opal had her sister's remains in an ugly, standard-issue crematory box on a shelf somewhere. How truly shameful!

CHAPTER 29

THE FAMILY MEETING

OPAL IS ABOUT to be picked up from her home to go to the office of attorney "Bob" Merson. She has never been to an important attorney's office before. Opal puts on her jury duty dress. It's a green, paisley polyester garb that only comes out of the closet for jury duty. The last time she did jury duty was fifteen years ago, so Opal is happy it still fits. She completes her ensemble with pantyhose under white anklets and her gray ankle boots. From inside a blue leather jewelry box, Opal finds a twenty-year-old gold lipstick tube. After applying the red color she blots her thin lips with a tissue.

Patty thinks this day is truly the worst day of her life. She and her retired sheriff ex-husband only have two vehicles between them, now: her beautiful Mercedes and Devon's shoddy old pickup. Patty didn't realize after Devon picked her up to go to Sizemore, they were going to fetch Opal, too.

Patty is sandwiched between the two people she hates most in the world. Devon reeks of a musky cologne he never bothered with when they were married. Opal smells like root beer and mothballs. Not one word is uttered between the three Highbrands on the chilly ride to Merson's office. Patty fidgets with radio selections that are mostly static while Opal makes the sucking sound you get with a mouth full of hard candy.

Janice is excited about going to Merson's meeting. She's curious as to how much money Devon, Patty, and Opal stole from Lois. Plus, Randolph just leased Janice a new Ford Explorer that she wants to show off to Patty.

Randolph threatened to back out of the meeting. The fact he was not consulted about the choice of attorney brought back all the old childhood bullying Devon did to him. Janice spent the morning convincing him they should go. Ultimately, Randolph decided she was right.

"Bob" Merson's outside, taking the last couple of drags off his cigarette when the Highbrands pull up all at once. Even in the bitter cold, Merson has his cowboy button-down opened to just above his beer gut. Merson's little charcoal branded shingle that identifies the occupant of this office on Main Street, has come unmoored from one hook and is flapping in the battering winter wind. Randolph and Janice wait in the warmth of their new vehicle until Opal, Devon, and Patty go inside.

Inside Merson's office are two leather wingback chairs, side by side in front of his large mahogany desk, with three folding chairs behind the leather chairs. Clearly, Merson expected Devon and Randolph to sit in the plush chairs, with the women in the folding chairs behind.

As he enters the office with Randolph and Janice, Merson sees Opal and Patty seated in the leather chairs. Devon is standing off to one side of the room. Janice sits down in one of the folding chairs, and Randolph stands on the other side of the room from Devon. Merson asks everyone if they want coffee. In unison, they all say, "NO!"

Merson eases into the session with some friendly banter. Opal impatiently interrupts Merson by asking him, "How can my sons stay as the executors of my sister's estate?"

Smiling at Devon's mother and with complete confidence Merson declares: "That will be easy!" Merson begins to explain his plan. "I know the three men on the Commission. I'm good friends with Maynard. They don't like …"

Before Merson can complete his sentence, Patty raises her right hand while adjusting her ivory cameo necklace with her left hand. Merson reluctantly acknowledges Patty, who blurts out, "Do we have to give back the money that Devon spent when he was Mallory's Power of Attorney?"

Devon is furious with his ex-wife for her idiotic interruption. Randolph and Janice knew nothing about Devon having access to Mallory's bank accounts. Randolph bursts out of his shell, yelling at Devon, "So that's how you fixed up your cabin!" Randolph looks at his mother. "You knew about this?" Randolph pauses to stare at the peculiar sight of his mother for a moment longer. He's never seen her with fire engine red lips.

Janice lights up. This is exactly why she wanted to be at the meeting. She taps Opal on the shoulder and whispers, "How much did they take?"

Before Opal can engage with Janice, Merson steers the discussion back to the county commissioners. He says, "Okay, let's focus on why we're here. The commissioners mainly like deciding who will be dog catcher and stuff like that. These types of disputes between family members never come before the commissioners. They don't like them. I'm going to send them a letter to dismiss and we'll wait for their response." Opal likes that idea, pivoting in her seat to give a nod and a smile to Janice. Janice silently motions to Opal to wipe the red off of her teeth.

Merson assures the room, "If the letter to dismiss somehow fails, then I'll just ask for continuances. The commissioners will grant me continuances for at least six months, probably a year, without asking for anything from Devon or Randolph."

Patty chimes in again, "Mallory is mentally impaired, with no abilities whatsoever. She is not doing this on her own."

Devon glares at Patty while agreeing, "We all know it's our cousin Amelia who's behind the petition." Affirmative mutters echo around the room, agreeing that Amelia Etchison is the real problem.

Janice says, "We don't even know her that well. She's always lived somewhere in California."

Patty adds, "She's never been married."

To which Opal exclaims, "And she has no brothers."

Merson assures everyone he will be denigrating their cousins, Amelia and Mallory, to the commissioners. He asks if anyone has any questions.

Randolph wants to know, "Am I in trouble for money Devon took from Mallory as her power of attorney? How much did he steal? That cabin didn't fix itself! And his wife has a new Mercedes!"

Devon glances at his brother and interjects, "We're divorced!"

Randolph fires back, "Then why is she here if she's not family?"

Patty snaps at Randolph, "Because I know a lot of things! And I'm not giving up my Mercedes!"

Devon tells Patty to zip it. He has no reason to suspect that Randolph knows about the trust fund being destroyed. The petition didn't elaborate on why the men should be removed from the estate. That will only come to light if Merson can't put a quick stop to the proceedings.

Merson senses the room could erupt. He explains to Randolph, "No one is in trouble. What Devon did when acting as Mallory's agent after her mother died has no bearing on what we're discussing here today. This petition only addresses removal of you and Devon as executors from your aunt's estate. But that's not going to happen."

Opal is satisfied, asking, "Are we done here?" She wants to leave before it comes out that she was acting as Mallory's agent, too. She doesn't know if the loose-lipped Patty knows about that. And her pantyhose are killing her.

Merson asks if anyone has any other questions. The room is silent. He ends the meeting by telling Randolph he might be in contact with him more often than Devon for signing affidavits, since he lives closer. Randolph thinks Merson is showing appropriate deference to him and has no objections.

As they stand to leave Opal informs Randolph she'll be riding back to Pine Hill in the new Explorer's backseat. She thinks Devon and Patty might have some arguing to do. Plus, once in the backseat of Janice's warm SUV, she plans to remove her pantyhose. Opal tells Randolph, "I have green beans and ham hocks simmering and I'm making meatloaf, mashed potatoes and cornbread for supper."

Merson overhears Opal's tasty menu and quips, "Can I come for supper?"

After Randolph, Janice, and Opal drive away, Devon grabs two cardboard file boxes out of the back of his truck that had been secured under a tarp. He sets them down inside Merson's office. It is all of Lois, Malcolm, and Mallory's entire paper history. All Merson can see from this trove of documents is dollar signs.

Just like during the old grifting days, Devon tells Merson, "Charge the estate as much as you can get away with!" Merson will kick back half to Devon.

Merson says, whispering so Patty can't overhear, "I'm charging $750 an hour. We'll each pocket $37,500 per every one hundred hours. I'll drag this probate matter out for at least a year."

CHAPTER 30

OPAL CAN'T SPELL

GLENDA THOMPSON HAAS seems competent enough to Amelia. She produced a legitimate, multi-paged power of attorney document, as opposed to Devon's two-page version, downloaded from "Legal Documents For Dummies."

When Amelia asked Glenda if Beasley County Commissioner Calvin Griffin, who's accused of airport theft, would be presiding over their probate case, Glenda's answer was, "Yes." When Amelia expressed concerns that the former sheriff is well known to the commissioners, Glenda soberly stipulated, "We'll have to see. It is unusual to remove executors named by a testator in her will."

Glenda's outlined to Amelia her case against the Highbrands for a complete breach of fiduciary duty. One, the executors changed the name of the beneficiary from "The Revocable Trust Of Lois Fleetwood," to Mallory Fleetwood. Executors cannot change a testator's chosen beneficiary. Two, the executors intentionally lied to Pinion Echo Bank and Trust, the testator's chosen trustee. The executors never funded Lois Fleetwood's trust, thereby destroy-ing her lawful trust. Trusts have certain protections. Three, the executors deliberately undervalued the estate on the appraisal with false dollar amounts and failed to submit the required non-probate form. Evidence backing these claims will be presented to the three panel commission when they issue a date for a Hearing On Petition.

After Opal received her "Revocation of Durable Power of Attorney" document from Glenda, Amelia received a nasty letter in the mail from her aunt. It was handwritten on Christmas stationery. At the top of each page was a manger scene with the three wise men keeping watch over the baby Jesus. It read:

> *"Amelia, I wish you would get the hell out of our lives! We went thru very trying times with Malory. Specialy Devon. No one has any inkling what he went threw. Oh, but he was mean to her when he would tell her to get out of bed, comb her hair, do her laundry that was piled high in the closet.*
>
> *"But of course the ones that do the least are the ones to complain. If she hadn't had money, no one would have given a dam what hapened to her. And then he couldn't handle her money and was stealing it. You know he was in the Marines Corp and was in charge of a hole lot of more money than she has. So I don't think we need your legal crap.*
>
> *"I think I know my sister a little better than you and Ann. She was my best freind and we shared everything our hole life. But somehow you and Ann knew her better. Did Lois tell you and Ann where she wanted her ashes spred? I don't think so. She showed me where she wanted them spred not buried. I didn't sugest doing it the summer after Lois died, as I didn't think Malory was up to it. Now she's gone. If Malory wants to go aginst her Mother's wishes we need to hear directly from her. We all have the phones you know. When you swoped in here like a theif in the night and took over we never knew who moved her or what hapened to her. So get a life and leave us*

alone! We will be waiting to hear from Malory if she's allowed to care. She knows our phone numbers as she called them plentey in the middle of the night.

Opal

"PS. I hope your happy that you drive a wedge between our familys."

Amelia realized when she read the letter that Mallory had reached out to her Aunt Opal for help and Opal turned her back on Mallory. Amelia sent Ann a copy of Opal's letter. They laughed about Opal's bad spelling. Ann showed it to her father. Eugene was disgusted.

Bud Wright installed the beautiful grave marker at the plot Eugene had arranged at the Arlodale Cemetery. Silas Cantwell brought Lois's ashes to the cemetery on that day, in a gorgeous rosewood burial box, just as he said he would. He placed a bouquet of flowers above the beautifully engraved headstone. Mallory finally got some closure about her mother's death. Two weeks before, Eugene mailed Opal a burial notice indicating the date and time of her sister's interment, in case she wanted to attend. Opal didn't show up.

CHAPTER 31

THE STANSBURY LAW GROUP

MADELEINE SIMONE STANSBURY grew up with the law. Her father is a lawyer. After Madeleine graduated law school, she joined her father's practice, the Stansbury Law Group. The Stansbury Law Group handles real estate sales, mostly. Madeleine's father, Carl, is also a realtor and property owner. Madeleine's work at the practice is general family law, mainly estate planning.

Madeleine contemplated dissolving the Stansbury Law Group as her dad approached retirement. She got her juris doctorate degree in Chicago, and always thought she'd head back to that city one day. She loves Chicago and thought she'd like to go into corporate trust litigation.

Madeleine's decision to work with her father seemed the safest after law school, and he'd offered her a sweet financial deal. She never anticipated living in the heart of Appalachia for ten years after graduating. But four years ago, she met someone in her hometown who wanted to stay there. So, Madeleine's now dug in, raising two kids.

The Stansbury Law Group is the advisory counsel for the

Beasley County Commission. The association between the two started over twenty years ago.

Carl got into professional trouble with the ethics disciplinary board. He wasn't one of the shady lawyers looking for the next scam. Carl genuinely thought he was helping an aged paraplegic when he counseled his widowed client to invest her car crash settlement into his property business for a six percent return.

Ada Pearl Rogers was referred to Carl after she was awarded a $66,000 insurance payment. Carl immediately put the funds into his attorney's trust account. From that account Ada asked for, and received from Carl, two payouts of $3,000 each. One check was for herself and one check was for her son. After those payouts, Carl advised Ada she should protect her money and invest the remaining $60,000.

The elderly woman didn't trust banks. So, Carl drew up a twenty-year contract between the Stansbury Land Corporation and Ada, which she signed. She would receive a monthly payment with the six percent factored in. Carl gave her a security interest in a piece of property, valued at $70,000, which exceeded the loan amount. However, when Ada demanded $31,000, eight months later, Carl couldn't comply because the loan money couldn't be liquidated. Ada filed a complaint against Carl Stansbury.

The ethics disciplinary board found that the transaction was not fair to Ada for several reasons, and ruled against Carl. One of several admonishments required by the board was for Carl to take on several pro bono cases. The Beasley County Commission was a pro bono job Carl kept through the years to reinstate his good name. With Carl retiring, Madeleine can end the association with the commission at any time.

"Motion to Remove Devon Highbrand and Randolph Highbrand as Fiduciaries for the Lois Fleetwood Estate" was sent to Carl by Maynard Fielding, the Beasley County Commission president. No probate matter had ever come before this commission panel wherein an heir was trying to remove the executors of a parent's estate.

Carl sent the case to Madeleine, telling his daughter they could quit as commission counsel immediately. Madeleine said she'd take a look and advise Maynard Fielding one way or the other.

After reading the petition, Madeleine decided the Stansbury Law Group should handle this one final case. Her advice to Maynard Fielding is to appoint a special fiduciary commissioner. Madeleine's offering her services since estate law is her specialty.

A week later, the Beasley County Commission sent an official notice to attorneys Glenda Thompson Haas and Q. Robert "Bob" Merson stating, "Special Fiduciary Commissioner, Madeleine S. Stansbury, Esq., is assigned to case #1472, Motion to Remove Devon Highbrand and Randolph Highbrand as Fiduciaries for the Lois Fleetwood Estate."

The first "ORDER" from Madeleine S. Stansbury, is to deny the request by Q. Robert "Bob" Merson that the case be thrown out. The second "ORDER" requires the executors to submit a final accounting of the estate prior to the Hearing On Petition in six weeks. Merson immediately replied to both "ORDERS" by asking for a continuance.

CHAPTER 32

"A GENTLE FOREVER SLEEP"

OPAL IS GLAD she socked away a big chunk out of Mallory's checking account before she was fired as Mallory's attorney-in-fact. Thirty thousand dollars will last her through the year, until her sons have free control of the estate again.

Opal knew Devon gave Mallory the first dose of fentanyl three months after he moved her to the downtown Perryville apartment. He'd taken fentanyl from the sheriff's lockup but wasn't necessarily planning to use it on Mallory. While Mallory's a problem, Devon and Opal never actually talked out loud to one another about outright killing her.

Devon stopped by Opal's one day, and told her he had just given Mallory a dose of fentanyl in a capsule. Opal didn't know what fentanyl was when he told her. But he was acting nervous about what he'd done. Devon explained to his mom, "I argued with Mallory this morning about taking her pills and doing her laundry. She wanted to go to the hospital for her nausea, and she said that her head hurt. She said she was calling an ambulance. I told her she was acting crazy and maybe she needed a check-up at the psych hospital. Then she screamed at me."

Sympathizing with her son, Opal said, "She is nothing but trouble. A hypochondriac, too."

Devon told Opal he left the apartment after Mallory screamed at him, just wanting to be done with her. The fentanyl had been kept hidden in a lock box in the back of his truck. Devon explained to his mom, "I told her the capsule would get rid of her nausea. I made her some tea to calm her down. She climbed back into bed. I left when she was sleeping."

The next morning when Devon returned to give Mallory her cocktail of prescription drugs, Mallory was up and about. That first dose of fentanyl didn't seem to harm her. He decided it worked to subdue her the same way it had quieted Lois. Each day, he might just give Mallory a tiny dose of fentanyl mixed with the regular prescription drugs. Devon prepped his mother by saying, "Maybe Mallory will just fall into a gentle forever sleep." Opal was only worried what could happen to her son if she did.

CHAPTER 33

"WHAT'S NEXT?"

"Bob" Merson's extremely worried about the appointment of a special fiduciary commissioner. It means the case is being fast-tracked. Commissioner Stansbury is doing nothing else for the commission except this probate case. Merson's plans for drawing this matter out for at least a year are ruined.

Merson doesn't know Madeleine Stansbury. He understood that her father, Carl, acted as the commission's legal counsel. Merson wondered why Carl didn't ask for the appointment of special fiduciary commissioner himself? Rather than wait for her response on his continuance request, Merson thought he should try to get a one-on-one meeting with Ms. Stansbury.

The Stansbury Law Group consists of two lawyers, Carl and Madeleine, and a law clerk. The Stansbury Land Corporation operates from the same office. Carl also employs a property manager and an accountant. They oversee his four-story office buildings in Claypoole. The two businesses share a receptionist.

Carl gave Madeleine an equal stake in the Stansbury Land Corporation when she joined the practice, but the agreement between them was for that corporation to provide retirement security and income. Now that her dad is drawing his retirement income, Madeleine can't borrow from the Stansbury Land Corporation to infuse the law practice. Soon, she'll have to contemplate bringing on another attorney to fill Carl's shoes.

One morning the receptionist buzzes Madeleine to say, "Robert Merson is calling."

Madeleine smiles. She isn't surprised "Bob" is calling, and says, "Put it through."

Merson introduces himself. He and Madeleine exchange the usual pleasantries. Madeleine tells Merson if he's calling about his continuance, he'll receive an official notice through commission channels.

Merson asks Madeleine, whom he addresses as "Commissioner," if he could have a one-on-one meeting to discuss the case. Madeleine advises that what he's asking is unorthodox. He should put his requests in writing to the commissioner to be presented to both parties. Madeleine hangs up with Merson knowing she will meet with him. She just wants to dangle him for a bit.

Later that afternoon, Madeleine emails Merson, stating,

> *"Mr. Merson, I decided a one-on-one meeting will be fine.
> I understand you reside in Sizemore, two-plus hours from
> commission headquarters. I'm in Claypoole, an additional
> half hour from Perryville. I suggest we meet in the middle, in
> McFarlane. There's a great little place for lunch, Gavin's Diner.
> I'd like to pick your brain on an unrelated matter. I'm tied up
> for the next two weeks. How is three weeks from today at noon?
> Regards, Commissioner Madeleine S. Stansbury."*

Three weeks later, they meet as planned at Gavin's Diner. Madeleine's seated when Merson arrives. Merson judges every woman under fifty by her appearance, and instinctively assigns a number from one to ten as soon as he encounters the opposite sex. Merson's brain immediately decided the commissioner is a strong eight. She's mid-thirties, very attractive with no makeup, and casually dressed. She has gorgeous, big eyes. Unfortunately, she wears a wedding band. The commissioner also sports a silver and turquoise bracelet. This is Merson's ice-breaker opportunity. He asks, "Where did you get that beautiful bracelet?"

They chit-chat while waiting for the waitress. Merson tells Madeleine he had a beautiful silver and turquoise bolero tie made while in the Army in Texas. Madeleine tells him about her work, and that her father is retiring. Merson puts that together with why Carl didn't take on the appointment of special fiduciary commissioner himself.

Madeleine discusses needing to bring on some fresh talent to the practice. She asks Merson if he has any ideas on who might want to join the Stansbury Law Group from over in Sizemore. Madeleine clarifies, "They wouldn't have to relocate to Claypoole."

Merson says, "I don't know of anyone offhand, but I'll ask around and get back to you." Merson removes his cowboy hat and places it in the booth next to him. A waitress named "Pammy" arrives and takes their food order. Madeleine excuses herself for a minute to take a peek at the selection of cakes and pies in the display case near the front door.

When the food comes, Merson's quite impressed that Madeleine ordered the french dip. She didn't care that the au jus was running down her chin, and that she had to wipe it away with a napkin after each bite. As he cuts into his chicken fried steak, Merson says, "I'd like to discuss the case."

Madeleine responds, "Sure. As soon as I finish my sandwich."

Uncharacteristically, Merson is a little intimidated by this woman's directness. So they both eat in silence for about five minutes, occasionally glancing up from their plates to look around the diner. As Madeleine pushes her empty plate to the side, she asks, "So, Mr. Merson, what did you want to talk about?"

Merson explains the probate case has no merit. His two clients are named as executors in the will. Executors don't get removed from estates and these are two very fine men, ex-Marines. He wants clarification as to why the commission accepted the case in the first place, and why the commission has declined to dismiss the case.

Merson knows the answer to the questions he's asking, but he has to cautiously advance to the reason for the meeting: his continuance. Plus, he wants to ascertain how pliable this woman is going to be going forward.

Madeleine gets right to the point of the matter. His clients changed the name of the testator's beneficiary. In the eyes of the law, that is a huge red flag. One of his clients was a county sheriff when the testator died. A trained sheriff is required to know how to settle an estate properly. She says, "Sheriff Highbrand submitted a false estate appraisal to Beasley County."

Madeleine leans forward and almost in a whisper, says, "Mr. Merson, it is obvious your clients had an ulterior motive for changing the name of the beneficiary to the daughter. If the decedent's money went into a trust they couldn't get their hands on it. The Highbrands are damn lucky this hasn't gone to the DA for a fraud probe." Madeleine sits back in her seat and continues, "If they are such fine men, why did they undermine their aunt's will? Your clients should resign. Just walk away from the estate, now!"

Merson is suddenly very defensive. He manages to say, staring her down, "My clients won't do that."

Madeleine asks about Devon's appraisal document, "Why was the estate appraisal less than $100,000?"

Merson shrugs as if he doesn't know why, even though he knows exactly why. He begins to speak, but Madeleine signals their waitress to come to the table. Madeleine orders apple pie and coffee and asks Merson if he'd like something. She asks him, "Have you tried their homemade pies?"

Merson wants to get out of there, but doesn't know if he should politely beg off while she's having dessert. He decides, instead, to speak to the commissioner as if he were speaking to a judge at trial. No more mister nice guy. He also puts his cowboy hat back on to signal he'll be leaving. He's sorry he politely removed it for her when he sat down for lunch.

As her fork slices through the first bite of pie, Merson reminds the commissioner that the estate is large. He insists his clients are ill-equipped for its administration, and are allowed to engage support. That's why they hired him. He'll need sufficient time to sort through the broad scope of financials to get a clear and accurate accounting. He doesn't believe her deadline is reasonable for the amount of work he has to do, and he has other clients, too.

Madeleine asks Pammy for more coffee, then quietly hits Merson with his reality between bites of pie and sips of coffee. She tells Merson, "I subpoenaed the entire, broad portfolio belonging to Lois Fleetwood. I've done your time consuming work for you. I'm aware of each money market, CD, savings and checking account that the decedent owned."

She tells Merson the estate was worth over $2 million at the date of death, a far cry from the $94,000 that was recorded by the county clerk. She reminds Merson, "You were only hired by your clients after a petition was filed for their removal. Your clients' refusal to "engage support" prior to the petition demonstrates their gross indifference to the estate."

Madeleine smiles as Pammy removes her empty pie plate. Merson is livid. He cannot believe this woman's verbal assault on his clients. He plans to call Maynard Fielding and get this woman removed as special fiduciary commissioner. Why is she saying all of this over lunch? Something seems off.

Madeleine educates Merson on the actual fact that a sheriff

who knowingly submits a false estate appraisal document is looking at misdemeanor charges. She also informs Merson she's aware of the $102,000 money market account that was cashed by Devon Highbrand. She's also aware of another account worth roughly $120,000 the former sheriff recently attempted to liquidate but he stupidly forgot to provide the death certificate. And, she finishes her analysis of the situation by stating, "I assume your clients would have plundered the entirety of the estate's portfolio had they not been stopped."

Merson tries very hard not to raise his voice to the commissioner as he explains, "The $102,000 account that was liquidated was a joint account. It was cashed in for the support of Mallory Fleetwood, and went into her personal checking account. All of that money was spent on things that benefitted the daughter."

Madeleine fires back, "Was giving fentanyl to Mallory Fleetwood for her benefit? Judge Crawford unsealed the APS report against Devon Highbrand, as I requested."

Merson is silenced. There's no possible retort to those last statements by the commissioner. He stares into the big brown eyes of Madeleine Stansbury while he adjusts to the information. Devon never mentioned an adult protective services case, or that he gave Mallory fentanyl. As a fiduciary, the commissioner is obligated to remand any such crimes to a district attorney for prosecution. Merson knows Madeleine has Devon on obvious misdemeanors. He realizes she could very likely convince the DA to charge attempted murder.

Madeleine disengages from Merson's stare and lets the facts sink in for a few minutes. Merson places his cowboy hat back on the booth next to him. She pays for their lunch during the interval and exchanges some friendly banter with Pammy.

When Pammy leaves, Merson asks, "What's next?"

Madeleine says, "I'm not referring your client to the DA for a felony indictment, yet. But Crawford has read the APS report, not just me. It's really damning. Glenda is only pursuing a probate matter, so far. This may not need to elevate to a criminal filing, provided you do exactly what I'm about to tell you to do."

The diner is empty of patrons. The short-order cook and Pammy are both in the kitchen. Madeleine asks Merson to hand her his jacket. He complies. Madeleine searches the pockets. She then tells him to get up and go to the back of the diner near the men's room. Merson is really curious why she's clearly looking for a recording device. Or maybe a gun? He says, "I'm not recording anything." Madeleine follows to the back of the diner.

After the pat-down Madeleine and Merson return to the table. For the first time in his life, Merson feels physically violated by a woman. Outside the men's room, she reached into his pockets and ran her hands up his inner thighs to his crotch. She bumped his abridged junk.

Madeleine says, "Hand me your phone." He looks at the commissioner with disgust and incredulity, then complies. Madeleine spells out his assignment. "Your clients never opened an estate bank account like they were supposed to when Mrs. Fleetwood died. You are going to tell your clients the probate assets will go into your lawyer trust account."

Merson interjects, "I don't currently have an open trust account."

Madeleine says, "Good. Because you're opening a brand new lawyer's trust. What did you do with your retainer for this case? Just cash it?"

Merson nods in the affirmative, then says, "Devon Highbrand will never go along with this."

Madeleine replies, "He doesn't have to go along." Merson's face displays confusion over her comment. Madeleine stares at Merson for a beat, then outlines the rest, "You and I will meet at the Charter Falls Bank branch in Perryville at ten a.m. tomorrow to open your new lawyer trust account."

Merson interrupts, "There's a Charter Falls in Sizemore. Can I just go there?"

Madeleine says, "No. What no one but you and I will know, is that I will be the second trustee. So, I need to be there. The trust will be titled "The 1472 Trust.""

Merson cagily asks, "May I please have my phone back so I can put this in my calendar."

Madeleine says, "No!" Then she continues with her instructions: "I've already drawn up the documents the bank will need. You have two weeks to put every probate item from nine different financial institutions into that trust account. The money's already been uninsured for over six months, so every penny better be there. How much are you charging in fees?"

Merson knows there is no point in lying to Stansbury because she has to approve his fees. Merson admits, "$750 an hour."

Madeleine laughs at his audacity, letting out an, "Oh my God!" After a beat she explains, "The executor fee will be $30,000. I'm allowing you to bill for your clients two percent on $1.5 million. That's roughly the total of all probate assets. I want Maynard Fielding to see I am being extremely deferential to you and Devon Highbrand. If I run into any problems, I'll be approving the very acceptable one percent executor fee, and you and your clients will get $15,000. Total!"

Before Merson can ask the most important question of all, Madeleine obliges with the answer. "Don't worry, Bob. I'm not going to leave you in charge of a trust fund for Mallory Fleetwood. As soon as Glenda sees the bottom line in the trust account, you'll legally resign as trustee. I've drawn up your resignation papers, too. At that point, I'll make the distributions. That's when you'll get your $30,000. Or $15,000."

Madeleine gives Merson his phone back, and says, "See you in Perryville." Merson puts on his cowboy hat and jacket and exits the diner without another word. Before leaving Madeleine points to a whole apple pie in the display case and says to Pammy, "I want to buy that one for my family."

On the drive back to Sizemore, Merson tries to figure out every way he can work around Madeleine's deal. He doesn't see a way out. If the Highbrand brothers had been court appointed executors, the decedent's assets would be required to go into a lawyer trust account. That's how he'll finagle the explanation to Devon. He'll tell Devon that because he changed the beneficiary and lied on the appraisal, the commissioner is requiring the money go into his lawyer trust account.

Merson really does want to protect his clients. Devon's in substantial legal jeopardy. He could do time. Randolph could be dragged through the mud. Merson realizes, too, if Devon's prosecuted, the grifting could come to light. It's close to four by the time he gets back to Sizemore. "Bob" is spent, so he just goes home and pours himself a huge scotch.

CHAPTER 34

GENERAL SHERMAN'S GHOST

IT WASN'T LOST on county residents who followed the postings of General Sherman's Ghost that once Devon was no longer sheriff, the blogger had gone radio silent. GSG kept the public guessing for years as to the identity of the sheriff department's most dogged critic. Even Merson noticed the absence of the culprit who labeled him, on more than one occasion, a "Coffin Chaser." Merson assumed General Sherman's Ghost was a man. He was half right. It was a man and a woman.

Calista Duke, or Cali as she is known around the county, is Angus Ungebuhler's youngest sister. She runs the big farmstand that the Ungebuhlers have along Mulberry Highway outside of Arlodale. The stand opens on the first day of April and closes the day after Halloween. When the stand closes, Cali travels the region to familiarize herself with which family farms can be ready with produce and pantry items to deliver to the stand the following spring. Some years they have over 100 vendors.

Her husband, Arnie Duke, is a local photographer and history buff who mainly does weddings. He also shoots the artwork for the billboard that will go up in March just beyond Arlodale, telling drivers the farmstand is two miles ahead on the right.

Arnie's younger sister is Melody Beverage. Her husband, Trucker, is Ramona Beverage's ex-husband. Melody and Trucker have custody of Ramona's two teenage girls. Trucker took the girls away from Ramona when she struggled with opioid addiction and took up with Wally Cotten a few years back. But Ramona is still part of the family and has become like a sister to Melody.

The Dukes were one of the victims of the grift scam created by Merson to exploit families of the deceased. Mabel Duke was Arnie and Melody's grandmother. She owned a century old, one-bedroom house with an attached little barn on the outskirts of Sizemore.

Arnie, Melody, and a first cousin, Kyle, were Mabel's only survivors, and they figured her estate was worth roughly around $40,000 at the time she died. No one wanted the tiny, rundown house, but the barn structure was still in fair shape and could be useful to someone looking to move to the area with a couple of horses. So, the three of them planned to sell the property and split the profits.

The sheriff told them to look up "Bob" Merson for a quick appraisal and settlement of the estate. Merson gave them an estimate for his services but they declined Merson's offer.

Arnie wrote up his own appraisal, which he gave to the sheriff to submit to the county. Arnie got a song and dance from Sheriff Highbrand that a legal appraisal couldn't just be done by a family member when the decedent dies intestate. Arnie asked if the heirs needed to do anything on the property while waiting for the sheriff to close the estate so it could be sold, such as pay the property taxes. Sheriff Highbrand said, "Nope, nothing needs to be done."

Less than four months later, the property was seized by the county assessor. Mabel had been in arrears on her property taxes for nearly five years before she died. Sheriff Highbrand either didn't know that or didn't care. He put the Mabel Duke estate settlement on the back burner because Merson wasn't hired to do the appraisal.

Mabel's house and barn sold at auction to none other than "Bob" Merson for $9,000. Arnie couldn't prove intentional wrongdoing by the sheriff, but the whole thing really stunk to high heaven.

So, Arnie and Cali created their online identity. Arnie had read everything about William Tecumseh Sherman. He thought a quote attributed to Sherman was ideal in their situation: "You get the enemy in the crosshairs and plug them, period!" Hence the name General Sherman's Ghost.

Cali already disliked Devon for disrupting her brother Angus's life. She and Arnie would blog about other topics that the county residents were focused on, too. But they were shocked at how much response their posts about Devon would get, and how the county really didn't like him and "Rotten" Cotten.

Cali and Arnie never informed anyone that they were General Sherman's Ghost. But one day, Melody told them about a huge marijuana field on the top of Dowd's Peak. They asked her how she knew about it. Melody said, "Ramona told me."

The Friday night Wally Cotten hooked up with Ramona, then bolted to go pick up Katy Legonick, Cotten told Ramona about the Dowd's Peak grow operation. Ramona confided in Melody the next day that she was upset that Wally left her apartment right after sex. So, she followed him that night. Ramona saw another woman get into his car at the West Run Creek bridge in Arlodale and he drove off with her. Ramona broke it off with Wally the next day.

Ramona didn't seen Wally again until his rape trial was getting underway. During the deposition phase at the Perryville Courthouse, Ramona overheard two FBI agents talking in the hallway. They had just deposed Sheriff Devon Highbrand, whom Ramona saw leaving the building. The men were talking about what the sheriff said under oath: "He didn't care if his deputy had sex with underage girls as long as he took it out of his county." Ramona heard the feds label Devon "a scumbag" before they ushered her into the room for her deposition.

Cali and Arnie are glad the county is clear of Sheriff Devon Highbrand, "Rotten" Cotten, and George Lee Welton III. They hoped their citizen commentary helped just a little bit! General Sherman's Ghost's final blog read, "Beer Gut 'BOB' chased the wrong coffin."

CHAPTER 35

THE REVEAL

MERSON CANNOT BELIEVE he has to get up and meet Commissioner
Stansbury at a bank. He's sorry he had that third scotch. He also
declines two calls from Devon on the drive to Perryville.

Madeleine is inside the Charter Falls Bank when Merson arrives
at 10:06 a.m. She's seated with Andy Nelson, the branch manager.
Over the next hour, they fill out the necessary papers to implement
the 1472 Trust. Quincy Robert Merson is named first trustee and
Madeleine Simone Stansbury is named additional trustee. A $10.00
deposit is made to open the account. Mr. Nelson gives each person
his card and thanks them for their business.

Madeleine hands Merson a large envelope. Madeleine says,
"These are Lois Fleetwood's financials. Shoot me a quick email
when you make each transfer to the trust!"

Merson replies, "Sure. What about the non-probate accounts?
I still need those to plug into the final accounting."

Madeleine responds, "It's all in there, probate and non-probate.
Everything Lois had on the date of death is in there."

Merson says, "Okay." He asks Madeleine if she is parked around the back.

She responds as she is texting, "No. My wife is picking me up."

Merson nods and smiles. He was not expecting that. His mind has to instinctively recalculate whether being in a same sex marriage elevates Madeleine past being a strong eight. The answer is yes. It vaults her to a nine, maybe a nine and a half depending on what the wife looks like. Merson pretends to adjust things in his briefcase. Without being too obvious, he lingers so he can exit the bank with Madeleine to get a glimpse of the wife.

Moments later, a blue Honda CRV pulls up and stops at the red curb in front of the bank. Merson and Madeleine exit together. Madeleine opens the door of the SUV. The woman driver leans over the passenger seat before Madeleine climbs in and yells, "Hi Bob!"

Merson squints to see who is greeting him. It's Debra F. Carver. He responds with a little wave before Madeleine climbs in and the door closes. Merson is left standing on the red curb with his mouth open as the car drives off. A beat later, the women look at each other and smile!!!

CHAPTER 36

THE RIFT OF THE GRIFTERS

THE SUN IS peeking through the blinds on a chilly morning. Devon is glad he has Mint in his bed, because everything else has collapsed around him. He didn't sleep at all. The words, "indicted on attempted murder," kept swirling around in his head as every hour ticked off through the night.

The phone rings, which wakes up Mint. It's Patty again. For two days she's been hounding Devon about the letter she received from Glenda Thompson Haas. It states that according to a ledger kept by Lois Fleetwood, Patty still owes $45,000 from her unpaid loan. Glenda's letter advises Patty to immediately begin $500 a month payments to Mallory Fleetwood. Devon ignores Patty's call.

The day before, Devon met with Merson at his office. Merson walked Devon through every aspect of his dim reality. He informed Devon he has no more control over Lois's wealth. Devon was livid. He accused Merson of fucking everything up!

Merson tried to interject some positivity as he outlined the payment structure that Devon will have to live with. He told Devon the executor fee is two percent, which is the very top percentage.

He mentioned the commissioner is being generous in that regard. Merson and Devon will split $30,000. Half of Devon's $15,000 goes to Randolph. The brothers will have to pay Mallory back for Merson's $5,000 retainer.

Devon scolded Merson for even suggesting they still divide the overall fee in half. He threatened to fire Merson. Merson told Devon he can do that. But the $1.5 million is already in the 1472 Trust. And Merson is the trustee. He also warned Devon that Commissioner Stansbury could easily turn this over to the DA if things don't go her way. He counseled Devon about the host of potential felony charges. Mallory is considered a vulnerable victim, and he was a sheriff and Mallory's legal agent when the crimes were committed.

Merson no longer sees Devon as his buddy. He's performing strictly as the Highbrand attorney, trying to get through this mess to the other side. Merson wants to be paid. If Devon is indicted, Merson wouldn't be his lawyer. He's not a criminal defense attorney. This is his last hope of seeing any money from the situation.

There were two things that Merson didn't tell Devon during their face-to-face. One was that Commissioner Stansbury is married to Debra F. Carver. Two: when it comes to being calculating, the commissioner is miles beyond anybody Merson's ever known.

When Merson opened the large envelope the commissioner handed him before they left the Charter Falls Bank, he saw that she had drawn up papers for Randolph to sign. Merson only needs to be the attorney-in-fact for one executor to retrieve Lois's assets without questions or obstacles. It avoids delays by any stupid people he might encounter at the varying financial institutions. The commissioner knew it would expedite things. Devon would never agree to give Merson control over the money. So, she prepared the attorney-in-fact documents for Randolph. Merson had to hand it to Commissioner Stansbury for her cunning.

Randolph was thrilled to learn he'll receive at least $7,500 from Lois's estate. He had no problem signing the documents

Commissioner Stansbury prepared. Merson became Randolph's attorney-in-fact and captured all of the probate assets without any hiccups. He funneled everything into the 1472 Trust.

CHAPTER 37
IT'S A BIG DEAL

IT IS EXACTLY thirteen days since Madeleine opened the 1472 Trust with Merson. Every penny of the roughly $1.5 million in probate assets is safely in the trust. Madeleine summoned Glenda Thompson Haas to the offices of the Stansbury Law Group the following morning. Madeleine told Glenda it could be a long meeting. She should carve out a few hours.

Glenda doesn't know Madeleine. But she had spoken to Carl from time to time around Perryville. Glenda was very curious what could require a long meeting. When she arrives at the Stansbury Law Group, Glenda compliments Madeleine on the beautiful office space. She asks if Carl is present that morning. She'd like to say hello.

Madeleine explains her father is retired from the day-to-day, and rarely comes to the office. Madeleine states that she is still completing some of Carl's work for him. It is one of the reasons she wanted to meet with Glenda. But Madeleine suggests they speak about the case before getting into Carl's business. Glenda is doubly curious, now.

Madeleine closes the door to the conference room. She begins by saying, "I should just present everything through commission channels. But this case is not one the commissioners want to deal with."

Madeleine pauses, then continues, "I had my own reasons for wanting to become the special fiduciary commissioner when I saw Devon Highbrand's name on your petition. Highbrand and Merson ran my wife out of her job a few years back."

Glenda exclaims, "What?"

Madeleine says, "Yeah. They forced her out as county prosecutor."

Glenda asks, "You're married to Debbie Carver?

Madeleine says, "Yup. We met about four years ago when she moved to Claypoole. Married a year."

Glenda says, "Congratulations! Doesn't she have little kids?"

Madeleine replies, "We do. Josie and Benjamin. Not so little anymore. Nine and eleven."

After a pleasant exchange over each other's kids, Madeleine continues, "When I told Fielding I'd act as special fiduciary commissioner, he jumped at my offer. He also told me he'd never agree to remove the Highbrand brothers from the estate. He's friends with Merson. They all know Devon Highbrand as a sheriff."

Glenda interjects, "I'm not surprised. These stupid county commissions. You get three, good ol' boys with zero legal training and unchecked power determining probate matters."

Madeleine agrees, "Yeah. Maynard makes a big show of having a public prayer session before each commission meeting. Yet he refuses to remove his crony who should be criminally charged for the improper handling of a dead woman's estate."

Glenda confesses, "I, I feel kind of responsible for this. I drafted the Fleetwood Trust. I should have told Lois Fleetwood to remove the brothers from her will at the same time she was removing them from her trust. It was before the Wally Cotten trial. I didn't know

Devon Highbrand or think a sheriff would be such a crook. I don't want to fail the daughter. I feel like I failed Lois!"

Madeleine reassures Glenda, "You didn't fail. This is a very unusual situation." Madeleine slides the Charter Falls Bank statement for the 1472 Trust in front of Glenda.

Glenda asks, "What am I looking at?"

Madeleine inquires, "So, do you think there is a fraud probe angle? Is Amelia Etchison considering criminal charges for fraud?"

Glenda replies, "A hundred percent not interested in a trial. Mallory was so traumatized by what she went through after her mother died, Etchison told me she could never be questioned again about anything that happened in Perryville. No. A criminal filing is out of the question. She's safe now. We just want the money."

Madeleine replies, "Okay. Do me a favor. Keep that to yourself, in case Merson asks you."

Madeleine explains to Glenda she is looking at a bank statement for a new trust fund titled the 1472 Trust. Madeleine says, "I need your help. I've protected all the money, but I could be disbarred."

Glenda asks, "Whose trust is this?"

Madeleine answers, "It's Merson's."

Madeleine walks Glenda through the situation. Madeleine explains, "I knew I could never trust Highbrand or Merson to report all of the estate's considerable assets. Merson's not only a crook, he's incompetent. When Merson asked for the continuance, I knew he wanted to slow the case down so he could charge more. It gave me time to subpoena everything before I'd have to respond to his request.

Glenda responds, "Thanks!"

Madeleine continues, "I can't trust the commissioners, either. Maynard Fielding will remove me as commissioner if Merson complains to him. I had to corner Merson, in such a way he'd do what I want him to do."

Glenda asks, "How'd you do that?"

Madeleine explains, "You sent me a written response to my 'ORDER' for the hearing on petition. Your letter stated Mallory couldn't attend the hearing due to a restraining order against Devon Highbrand, pursuant to an APS case filed by the Clyburn Clinic. I asked Judge Crawford to unseal the adult protective services case. I had no idea there was an APS case until you sent that letter."

Glenda responds, "I wanted to explain to you who Mallory is and why she can't come to the hearing."

Madeleine says, "That was my leverage over Merson. The possible charge of attempted murder for giving Mallory Fleetwood lethal drugs. That's why I don't want Merson to think a felony referral is off the table."

Glenda agrees, "I understand. May I have a copy of the APS report?"

Madeleine says, "Of course. She had fentanyl in her bloodstream. He was basically forcing pills down her throat every day. There could have been an indictment if she didn't move away!"

Glenda shakes her head. "Poor thing!"

Madeleine points to her name as trustee on the 1472 Trust bank statement, and continues, "So, I had Merson funnel all the probate assets into a special lawyer's trust. I made myself a trustee. Now that you've seen that every penny of probate inventory is in here, Merson is going to resign as trustee. I'll be in charge of the account."

Glenda responds, "Wow! Highbrand didn't object to a lawyer's trust?"

Madeleine shrugs. "I don't know. I have no idea what Merson told the ex-sheriff. But clearly, you can see why I could be disbarred for all of this."

Glenda answers, "Could you, really? The account's only for this case, right? You are the fiduciary."

Madeleine responds, "I don't know. But I wouldn't want to take it out for a spin with the current ethics disciplinary board."

Madeleine points to the bank statement. "This is your copy for Amelia Etchison. Let me call Merson. He knew you were coming here this morning. Help yourself to coffee and food in the kitchen. I'll just be a minute!"

Madeleine speed dials Merson's number. "Hi Mr. Merson. Good. How are you? Good. Glenda's here with me. She's seen the account. Thank you for getting everything deposited." Madeleine listens as Merson explains he'd like to bill sooner than later. Madeleine responds, "Andy Nelson has been told you'll be submitting your resignation papers today. I'm going to talk to Glenda about canceling the hearing in a couple of weeks. That'll get everyone paid sooner. I'll send an 'ORDER' out to Maynard Fielding to immediately close the estate. I'll make the final distributions."

Amelia received a text with a photo of a bank statement from Glenda. The message said,

> *"I'm meeting with Commissioner Stansbury. All of Lois's assets are safely in this trust account. We'll speak later."*

Before seeing the text, Amelia didn't know how much money Lois had in probate assets. Even though Lois gave a list of financial institutions to Gail Bowers, there were no dollar amounts indicated on the list. What an enormous relief for Mallory's future security!

Amelia had been thinking about how all the events unfolded after Lois's death. All of this theft and abuse might have been avoided if Leeland Culp had said something to his bank's legal department. Culp knew what Lois was worth. Did he really believe there was no money for a trust fund? Pinion Echo Bank and Trust was not going to get another crack at handling Mallory's finances.

Amelia texts Glenda back,

> *"This is amazing. Thank you! Been thinking. Mallory may not need a special needs trust. Let's talk about possibilities. Also, any response from Patty Highbrand after your letter?"*

Glenda replies,

"No response from Patty. And yes, absolutely. Be happy to help you and Mallory if I can."

Along with the $1.5 million, Amelia had already secured another $300,000 in non-probate accounts where Mallory was named as the survivor beneficiary. She'd need to decide if it's worth the hassle of going after Devon and Opal for the money they stole from Mallory's checking account. More importantly, soon Amelia would have to figure out an investment strategy for Mallory's $1.8 million!

CHAPTER 38

MALLORY TOWERS ABOVE IT ALL

Four years later …

THE ABANDONED DURBIN and Kern Tannery complex that sat vacant for decades was bought by the Stansbury Land Corporation. The old ghost town of seven buildings was torn down. The name on the stone wall just beside the iron gate that allows entrance to the brand-new industrial complex reads, "FLEETWOOD TOWER COMPANY, a subsidiary of Fitzgerald/Bosley Communications." Finally, there are a few more jobs for the citizens who live in and around Pine Hill.

"Chatty" Patty Highbrand is the recently hired daytime receptionist at Fleetwood Tower Company. On condition of employment, $500 is deducted out of her salary each month to pay off her old debt to Lois. The automatic deposit goes into the bank account of Mallory Fleetwood.

Four years earlier …

Madeleine walks to the kitchen to get Glenda. She announces, "Merson's on his way to Perryville to resign as trustee. Let's go back and sit down. Something else I want to discuss with you."

Glenda grabs her cup and a pastry. As she follows Madeleine back to the conference room, Glenda remarks, "Great cappuccino machine. I sent Amelia Etchison a text of the trust statement."

Madeleine responds, "Great! I think we can just cancel the hearing on petition, don't you?"

Glenda replies, "Oh, sure. If you think we can. That would be great."

Madeleine says, "Fielding won't question anything as long as I tell him to close the estate, but don't technically remove the executors. Merson's already agreed. It'll save everybody some money. I'll send out an 'ORDER' tomorrow. Then we're done. I'll make the distributions."

Glenda asks, "How much is Merson charging?"

Madeleine responds, "I capped the executor fee at $30,000. It's two percent."

Glenda says, "I'll need to see what Amelia wants to do."

Madeleine says, "I may have an idea. I mentioned my father has been working on other business. Are you familiar with Fitzgerald/Bosley Communications?"

Glenda replies, "Sure. They're a phone company. They're not in Beasley. Not yet, anyway."

Madeleine clarifies, "Not just phone. They've been around for seventy-five years. They service everything, internet, TV, land lines, cell service. They were one of the first to provide DSL to any part of Appalachia."

Glenda nods. " Huh. Interesting."

Madeleine continues, "My father got into trouble with the ethics disciplinary board years ago. He was required to take on several pro bono cases. That's why he had the Beasley County Commission."

Glenda nods and responds, "I see."

Madeleine smiles and continues, "Carl also had Fitzgerald/ Bosley as a pro bono case, years ago, when they were still a user-owned collective. Decades back, they wanted to bring cell service into Beasley. My dad tried to broker deals for private landowners to build cell towers, but there wasn't any money in it back then. Carl's been approached about a partnership opportunity with Fitzgerald/ Bosley. From his pro bono days, Dad's remained good friends with one of the owners, Domnhall Fitzgerald, or 'Fitz' as we call him."

Glenda interjects, "Sounds exciting!"

Madeleine continues, "Fitz got advance notice about a trillion dollar infrastructure investment. He's been pushing for expansion in Appalachian technology and telecommunications for forty years. This particular four-year proposal connects broad areas to the eastern and northern metropolitan corridors, with new highway systems."

Glenda responds, "Wow!"

Madeleine says, "Fitz wants Stansbury Land Corporation to buy up the affordable parcels of land that Fitzgerald/Bosley has mapped out along the expansion zones. He also wants us to build the cell towers. Fitzgerald/Bosley provides the connectivity. The mapped parcels are still cheap. But they won't be for long."

Glenda says, "Fascinating! Can we pause for a minute? That delicious cappuccino went right through me."

Madeleine says, "You bet. Restroom's by the front door." Madeleine is glad for the break. She feels like she is just babbling and wasting Glenda's time. She needs to get to the point of why she's telling Glenda all of this. She wants to invest Mallory's inheritance into the Stansbury Land Corporation for the merger.

It's frigid outside and it has started sleeting. Merson hopes this is his last trek to Perryville for a while. As he leaves the warmth of the Charter Falls Bank after handing Andy Nelson his resignation papers, it really hits him. Debra F. Carver must be so satisfied that her wife has bested him. Merson muses out loud as he drives back to Sizemore, "It woulda served Carver right if I fucked over her wife. I shoulda taken all the money and headed to Mexico."

For the next several minutes, Merson imagines himself living the life in San Miguel de Allende as a wealthy American ex-pat. He pictures himself with wife number four who's at least a number nine. On the patio of his sizable hacienda they'll do tequila shots with friends each afternoon. Maybe he'll write his memoirs at night. His wardrobe will change from Texas classic to t-shirts, cargo shorts, and flip-flops. He'll drive a Vespa through the streets to the cigar shop. Then BAM …

Merson is awakened from his enticing daydream when a deer jumps in front of his vehicle. He instinctively slams on the brakes, barely missing the frightened animal whose hooves have no traction on the icy road. But he's now hydroplaning sideways and backwards down the middle of the slippery asphalt. Merson has zero control. His SUV comes to a stop on its side in a steep ditch on the other side of the road.

Merson is unhurt but there's no cell service on that side of the mountain. With all his might, he forces open the driver's side door enough to shimmy up and climb out into the freezing air. The door closes behind him. Merson tromps around the muddy ditch. He soon realizes after assessing the situation, now that he's outside the upended vehicle, that he can't get back in. Merson and his wreck are immediately hit by a barrage of heavy wet snow.

Four years later …

As Devon holds his wife's hand at the obstetrician's office, look-ing at the ultrasound of the fetus Mint's carrying, he can't believe he's starting over with a new family. The nursery will be the extra bedroom in his old cabin where they reside.

Mint works at the Fleetwood Tower Company, which is just

up the road. Devon drives Mint to and from work each day so he can have the use of her car. Devon's old pickup is a rusted junk heap in the field behind the cabin. Twice a day he sees the giant letters spelling FLEETWOOD TOWER COMPANY before the exceptionally slow motorized gate opens, allowing entrance to the five-acre complex. After dropping Mint off, Devon heads to the men's club hall. He unloads deliveries, assists the daily cook with chopping, and cleans the tables after the seniors have had their hot lunch. He eats a meal if there's food left over. After that he drives old Pesky Fleming over to Arlodale to Harvey's Guzzle-N-Gulp which is now run by Harvey's son, Greg. They each buy five lottery tickets and loaf a bit outside on nice days before Devon has to pick up Mint. Pesky has no teeth to whistle through anymore.

Alan is home from the Air Force and works as a tower climber for Fleetwood Tower Company. He also trains wannabe tower climbers. He now lives in Patty's hilltop dream home with his wife and two kids. The sixty acres is still in his name.

Patty asked her son to give her back the land and the house, but his wife wouldn't allow that. So, Patty still resides in her hilltop dream home, with Alan and his family, although her bedroom is now Catherine's old room.

Devon approached Alan, too, about dividing up the sixty acres. Devon wants at least ten acres with the cabin parceled off for him and Mint to own. But Alan's wife Felicity stood firm against that, too. So, Alan lets Devon and Mint reside in the cabin for free, but only until after the baby comes. At that point, Felicity plans to turn the cabin into an Airbnb for visiting climbers. She doesn't care much for her morally bankrupt father-in-law and his new wife. Her daughters aren't allowed to be around their grandfather.

Opal cooks breakfast, lunch, and supper every day for Randolph, because she lives with him. After her thirty thousand dollars ran out at the end of that first year, she was broke. She used the profits from selling her property to pay off Randolph's mortgage and improve his home.

Janice loves having a full-time cook, housekeeper, and babysitter. Randolph and Janice ended up with an "OOPS" baby four months ago, conceived as Janice entered early menopause. They named him Owen which means young warrior. Now, like Patty, Janice has four kids.

Opal only sees Devon at church every Sunday since she lives with Randolph. She adores his second wife. Mint takes Opal shopping and buys her root beer hard candy. On their last outing Opal made Mint a promise: "I will still love you even if you give birth to a daughter!"

Madeleine and Debbie are in Las Vegas with their two kids for a tween queen concert. Josie is obsessed with pop star Kendall Perry. Benjamin made them promise he'd get to see his favorite magician. They took the early flight from Chicago Saturday morning so the kids didn't miss school on Friday.

At a bar at the Sun City Hotel and Casino, while Josie and Benjamin are watching an afternoon movie, Madeleine and Debbie give a nod to "Bob" Merson, who froze to death on a desolate stretch of country road exactly four years ago. Madeleine says, "His tragedy won't happen again."

Debbie agrees, "Thanks to you!"

Madeleine corrects her, "Thanks to Mallory." They clink their cocktail glasses and make a toast: "To Mallory!"

When "Bob" Merson died unexpectedly, Madeleine's distribution of the $30,000 executor's fee for Lois Fleetwood's estate was paid to Merson's law practice, Cowpokes Kick Legal Ass, PLLC. Had he lived, Merson would have divided up equal payments to Devon and Randolph after taking his fee. But, he didn't live. Oddly enough, Merson died without a valid will. His estate went to probate court. Randolph was the only executor who was able to show the court that Merson had indeed performed as Randolph's attorney-in-fact for the administration of the Lois Fleetwood estate. Devon and Merson had nothing in writing indicating an attorney-client relationship. Devon was also convicted on a misdemeanor charge for submitting a fraudulent estate appraisal while he was a sheriff. Therefore, the portion of the executor fee that would have been divided equally between the brothers all went to Randolph. It was Randolph's responsibility if he wanted to give Devon his share. That never happened.

Amelia is on her way to a couple of corporate events out of state. She thought the two-day journey into the middle of Appalachia was behind her when she moved Mallory to San Diego. Now, it's a twice-a-year excursion to the Fleetwood Tower Company as the company's vice president, and then on to Fitzgerald/Bosley Communications where she'll attend a board meeting. But it's been fun.

Amelia stays with Ann and Ned when she gets to Pine Hill. Sadly, Eugene passed away two years ago. He lies near Payne and Lois in the Arlodale Cemetery. Opal didn't attend his burial, either.

On this visit, Fleetwood Tower Company is throwing a one hundredth birthday bash for old Estes Durbin. The offices in the Fleetwood Tower Company buildings are decorated for the occasion with blown-up vintage photos from Estes Durbin's life. Everyone's favorite picture is Henry Durbin next to his moonshine still. Estes is the five-year-old in the picture, drinking something from a tin cup.

The purchase of the abandoned Durbin and Kern Tannery complex was one of the first acquisitions by the Stansbury Land Corporation after their merger with Fitzgerald/Bosley Communications. It was the ideal site as a centralized headquarters for Fleetwood Tower Company. The state of the art complex is used to train climbers who come from all over the region. Estes let it go for pretty cheap. He also sold three acres on his Dowd's Peak property to Stansbury Land Corporation to put up two towers and a relay building. Cell service from one of those guyed towers could have prevented the death of "Bob" Merson on that back mountain road. The road got closed the day he died due to blizzard conditions. No alerts could reach Merson and he could not phone anyone for help to say he was stranded.

Estes kept the two acres he's been leasing to Craig Cutler for the last eighteen years. Craig's in his will to receive those two acres when Estes dies. Estes has always been opposed to marijuana being illegal. Freddy Hoover, who's into his second term as sheriff, doesn't police private properties in his county for marijuana grow sites. And when Freddy needs to acquire more pot for his wife's kidney cancer, he doesn't need to honk at Finn's. Finn just brings it by Freddy's home. Cutler, Finn, and Freddy will be at Durbin's birthday party.

Domnhall Fitzgerald doesn't know Mallory Fleetwood personally. But he was incredibly impressed that this woman helped enable his partnership with the Stansbury Land Corporation to fulfill his vision of expanded telecommunications throughout a forgotten portion of the country. Mallory's $1 million, combined with Carl's $2 million, was enough to begin the crucial site purchases in key locations along the highway expansions.

Six months later, when Fitzgerald/Bosley Communications received its $490 million subsidy from the Appalachian Infrastructure and Telecom Investment Fund, he returned Carl and Mallory's seed money. He bought out the southern based Dixieland Tower Company. It was unanimously decided by Fitzgerald/Bosley Communications and the Stansbury Land Corporation to change the name of their new acquisition to the Fleetwood Tower Company. Ninety percent of the targeted expansion has been completed. All of the nationwide carriers are tenants throughout the region.

Mallory loves living in her cute condo in San Diego near Amelia. She enjoys taking the Paratransit bus to adult day care five days a week. She helps the staff hand out the morning and afternoon snacks. Her favorite day for lunch is taco Tuesday and she's the loudest voice during the daily sing-alongs. When Amelia's out of town, Mallory's personal attendant comes to stay with her.

Mallory is a profit participant in the Fleetwood Tower Company. She doesn't know too much about that. But she loves telling people she owns a few cell towers which provide safety and communication to people in Appalachia where her mother was raised. Mallory's tower leases bring in $183,600 annually, so far …